## BLACK FLAMINGO

In Africa, the black flamingo signifies that the Azande tribe will once again be powerful.

Two men have ended up in the middle of nowhere, due to a crashed jeep and a crashed aeroplane. Bill Sinclair meets Bill Hadlow briefly before Hadlow dies from malaria and he takes on his identity, removing his passport, pilot's licence and other belongings.

Bill struggles from the hills into a village where he is treated by the local witch doctor, N'Dene and he meets Nina and her step-father. This is just the beginning of his involvement with the diamond trade, of his new identity and his relationship with Nina.

# BLACK FLAMINGO

## Victor Canning

·BLACK·
DAGGER
·CRIME·

First published 1962
by
Hodder & Stoughton

This edition 2001 by Chivers Press
published by arrangement with
the author's estate

ISBN 0 7540 8597 X

Copyright © 1962 by Victor Canning

**British Library Cataloguing in Publication Data available**

Printed and bound in Great Britain by
Bookcraft, Midsomer Norton, Somerset

# CHAPTER ONE

THERE was little light yet; only a soft greyness that hazed the distant line of mountains. Over the lake there was a thin mist that the before-dawn breeze swept slowly upwards so that it wrapped itself high about the tree trunks on the slope below the homestead and swirled lazily across the hard-packed earth between the huts.

N'Dene came to the door of his hut and shivered a little with the freshness of the morning air. He reached down and dipped a half gourd into the closely plaited water basket. He filled his mouth, rinsing the water over his teeth and tongue, and then blew it out in a fine spray to take the taste of the night from him. He was an old man, shrivelled, his skin hanging deflated and slack over his tall bony frame. He scratched his belly gently, just above the thong that held his bark cloth apron. With age, he thought, even a man's bones seemed to shrink and the skin hung on them like the hide of a wasted antelope. In his youth and in his manhood there had been muscle, rippling and hard, under the close-grained chocolate skin. Now, he was a shell, filled with nothing but memories.

He moved slowly across the sandy earth between the huts. In the middle of the open space was a piled earth mound into the top of which had been stuck a large forked stick. This was the *tuka*, his family ghost shrine. Somewhere in the tree tops down by the lake a red monkey, as cold as he was, woke and began to scream angrily for the sun. And on great soft wings a *huba* owl went by on its last foray.

N'Dene began to climb the slope above the homestead as he had done for more mornings than he could remember. In a little while the village would be awake and the women

5

and children would go off to their work on the cleared
ground near the lake where the eleusine crop was good this
year. He began to think of food, but not of eleusine, nor
maize, nor cassava nor ground nuts, but of meat. A little
saliva formed in his mouth. He spent most of his time
thinking either of food or of the past, and the past beyond
his own past. But memory brought regret, and never
more so than at this time of the morning when he went up
the hill above the homestead. It would be good to be
young again, to be a warrior and to take his place in the
*apalanga* of a chief, to have the strength to fight, to have the
teeth to enjoy meat, to drink eleusine beer and dance and
know again the quick, loin-sharpening joy of wanting and
taking a woman. Twenty throwing spears he had given
for his first wife. But she had not been his first woman. He
tried to think back to that first but the memory escaped
him.

High above the homestead was an old thorn tree, iso-
lated in the waste of rocks and scrub, and below it a flat
stretch of stone which made a seat for him. N'Dene sat
down and turned his face to the lake and to the east. The
grey water mist over the lake's surface stretched away for
miles to the north, cupped by the surrounding mountains.

Slowly with the coming of the morning the mist was
sucked upwards, thinning and disappearing. A bird came
and sat on the thorn and scolded him and, far away across
the bare slope, he saw a pack of baboons going rapidly up
the hillside; and from the trees below the homestead he
could hear the red monkeys howling now with frenzy for
the sun. Since his boyhood he had known this lake and
these mountains, and for many years now, since he had
become an old man, he had risen before all the others and
come here each morning to watch the sign of the Azande
greatness, the living totem of his tribe. Many memories
went through his mind as he sat there waiting for the sun.
... It was up here, farther along where the termite
mounds were, that as a young man he had met for the first

and only time a cat woman, a bad woman who was full of witchcraft and had had relations with a wild cat of the kind called *adandara*. She had been walking along a path followed by the two kitten she had borne, one female and the other male. The male had been easy to recognise for it had carried a bunch of charms around its neck. And when he had got back to his hut he had become dizzy and sick and could not lift his arms. But the woman had come to him and explained that as he, too, had witchcraft in him, good, cool witchcraft, she did not wish to harm him and would cure him of his sickness. She took hold of his arms and made him rise, then she told him to crawl from behind her between her legs. He did so and he was cured. But her name he told no one. Oh, there were many things he remembered, many things he had seen . . . he, N'Dene of the Azandes.

The sky was lightening rapidly now and the mist going. He could see the waters of the lake, stretching for miles until it was lost against the far mountains. A string of small green islands marked the lake and around the islands where the water was shallow, drying out sometimes in the great droughts, he could see the warty mud piles pocking the surface, the nests of the flamingoes.

The sun tipped the far mountain crests and around him the stippling of felspar in the granite was fired by the sun's rays. He raised his face to the sun and watched the lake. In a moment it would happen. He watched now, knowing exactly where the first shaft of sunlight would touch the lake. One moment it was not there, and next it was like a hand spread over the grey water. He sat there, rapt, as the sun slowly put life and brightness into the water. Slowly at first the flamingoes began to move, to thrash clumsily for a while over the water and then take off on their morning flight. They went in twos and threes and then, gathering in a great company, sweeping round low at first, confused and without order, suddenly merged into a drilled, disciplined flight, circling in a pink and white

haze over the grey-green, silver-flecked water. They rose
higher, their wings catching the sun, wheeling and streaming into the sky, making a great cloud over the lake so that
the whole sky was pink and white and wing-broken. And
at their head, as always, flew the one black flamingo, leading them, the sign of his tribe's greatness, the bird of
M'Bori. . . .

N'Dene sat there watching the morning flight and there
was a great happiness in him. What did the young men of
the tribe today know of these things? Was it not he,
N'Dene, who had told even their chief, their prince
Mabenge, of these things? And Mabenge had listened. It
is I, he thought, who have told Mabenge of these things
. . . of the great days of the past before there was a white
man in this country, of the greater lake than even this one,
the lake far, far to the north where their peoples once lived
and then were driven out by the men in white robes from
the desert. The Avungara and the Azande had been
driven from the north and had come south to conquer and
to prosper under their kings and princes. All this he had
told Mabenge; of King Gura and his sons Tombo and
Mabenge, and how they had become kings, too; and of
Yapiti the second son of that distant Mabenge who had
brought his people to the Uele river and of King Bainbi
after Yapiti and then King Gbudwe. . . . All these things
he knew, when the young men of the tribe today knew
nothing except to scratch themselves when they itched and
had no more memory in their heads than there was between the fork of their legs. But Mabenge, although he
had lived in distant countries, had listened and questioned.
And why should he not? Of all the Azande Mabenge was
the greatest. The blood of King Gura ran through him.
Long ago, it had been the first son of Gura, himself named
Mabenge, who had brought them here, before he lived,
before his father or his grandfather lived, but the memory
was in N'Dene as truly as the blood was in Mabenge.

Below him the morning flight was dying as the birds

settled back to the lake and their feeding grounds. And N'Dene watched and saw again, as he had seen so many mornings, that the last bird to desert the sky, the last to settle and feed was the black flamingo of the Azande.

He got up from his stone and went stiffly down towards the homestead where he would sit in the shade of the hut and his favourite grandson, one of many, would bring him his smoking pipe and keep him company while the women worked.

\* \* \*

Mabenge stood behind the set looking down at Major Winton. An Azande was at the door of the hut, naked except for the *roko* about his loins. The sweat glistened on his shoulders. Beyond him the valley was full of hard, biting sunlight.

"Come in, Oracle! Come in, Oracle!"

Winton threw the key and waited. There was only the faint crackle of static, a whisper under the grass roof of the hut.

Winton looked up at Mabenge and the lean, sun-tanned face wrinkled with anger and impatience. He beat one hand impetuously on the side of the small table.

"Why the hell doesn't he answer?"

"He's been in every half hour for the last hour and a half," said Mabenge. He knew Winton too well to try and curb his impatience. Nobody could do it. When his temper went he became a ball of fire. Put your hand on him and sparks flew as they did from a stroked cat.

"Then why the devil isn't he in now?"

Winton threw the key and spoke again.

"Oracle, come in. Oracle. Oracle. Damn you, Oracle, come in!"

The key went over and again the static whispered gently. Winton picked up his empty pipe and jammed it in his mouth. One day, thought Mabenge, who wasn't without humour—though at this moment he shared all Winton's concern—he would jam it right down his throat by mistake. But he would probably swallow it without noticing it. Little beads of sweat shone above the line of Winton's thin, dark moustache, and his face worked furiously as he chewed at the pipe.

Suddenly the static ceased whispering and crackled up like a sudden flare of burning twigs and from the heart of the noise a voice ghosted into the room.

"Prophet. Prophet. Oracle here. Are you getting me, Prophet? Out."

Winton threw the key.

"Prophet here, Oracle. We're getting you. Where the devil have you been? Out." The key jerked over.

The static roared like a bed of pebbles on the move.

"Oracle here. Keep your hair on, Prophet. I've got my hands full here. Electrical storm and rain. A real first-class job. And I'm in trouble. What do you make me from you? Out?"

Winton grabbed at the key and was talking fast after a glance at the map on the table at his side.

"Oracle. Oracle. I make you about a hundred miles north of Lisala. You should be crossing the Ebola any time. And that puts you about a hundred from us. You should be here in less than two hours easily. Over."

There was no static this time and the ghost voice filled the hut with a startling robustness.

"O.K. Prophet. But corrections. This thing is a dead duck. I can't make back to Lisala. Too dangerous, eh? And there won't be any Ebola crossing. The elastic's gone somewhere in the motor and I can't do anything about winding it up. There's nothing below me but trees and I'd tear myself to pieces on them. Don't fancy it. Whoah! There she goes again . . ."

The room split suddenly with a roar of static and Mabenge saw the jerk of Winton's cheek muscles. The roar petered away into a long rushing sound and then the voice came back.

". . . Some guy up here wants to tear my wings off. The Ebola's below me, but I'm not crossing it. I'm going up it. Now listen, Prophet . . . Listen hard. This is my neck and I like it the way it is. There's no landing among the trees and I'm losing height fast. I'm going up the river and picking a sandbank. Plenty of 'em. I'll pick one and come down off the tail end in the water. Should manage it. But you'll have to come out for me. If I make it in one piece I'll go up the river on foot and head north for you. But I don't fancy the walk alone so come out for me. Don't worry. Over."

Winton thumbed the key viciously.

"Oracle. Oracle. Stay with the plane until we come. Stay with it. Over."

The static gossiped unintelligibly in the hut. Winton glared at the set as though it were a personal enemy and Mabenge watched him, knowing what was going through his mind, and himself already making calculations.

The voice came back.

"There isn't much room down there. But I think I can make it. But don't expect me to sit on my bottom waiting. Somebody may see me come down and Lisala isn't much farther away than you. I've come too far to risk anything at this moment. I'll walk on. It isn't only the storm. Must have been bloody watered petrol at Coquihatville. Here we go, and fingers crossed. . . ."

The voice died and the static whispered and crackled.

Winton tried two or three more times to raise the plane but there was no answer. He got up from his seat and walked to the door of the hut and back.

He was a man of about fifty, small, compact, with the figure of a jockey. His dark eyes shone angrily in the hard face which was brown and creased like a drought-dry lake bottom. When he moved there was a wiry restlessness in him as though every moment was precious to him, that there was work, too much work for him to do, and always somebody trying to hold him back, always somebody getting in his way. He wore a bush shirt and breeches with puttees and looked as though he would be uncomfortable in anything else. He stopped in front of Mabenge and ran one hand through his iron-grey hair.

"Well?"

Mabenge smiled.

"We shall find him."

"He could kill himself."

"It's not likely. Hadlow is a man of experience."

"Why the devil did it have to happen on the last lap?"

Mabenge shrugged his shoulders. He shared all Winton's apprehensions, but in his own nature—while equally determined—there was a philosophical resignation. Life was full of accidents. One accepted them and adjusted oneself to them.

"It was better to happen on the last rather than the first lap, no?" His voice, educated, had a slight singing note when he spoke English. He was much taller than Winton, straight, slim, but well-muscled about the chest and shoulders which gave his body a long, athletic, wedge shape, tapering away to his feet. His face was round, nearing plumpness, with a wide mouth whose lips were thick and somehow put the rest of his features out of proportion. His dark skin seemed very dark because of the shining, almost purple underbloom characteristic of his race. He wore linen trousers, a loose shirt, and his feet were bare.

Winton reached for his pipe from the table and began to stuff it from his pouch, his fingers ramming the tobacco home hard.

"We've got to find him."

"We will. It might take us a week to get down there. How many men?"

"Three or four. We want to go fast and light. And until we go have a man on here every half-hour. He might come through. And as we go you can spread the word for your people to look out for him in all the homesteads." He picked up the map. "That part of the Ebola is in Ngbandi country, isn't it?"

"It is. But they are part of my people. We may be gone for two weeks. What will you tell Miss Nina?"

"As little as possible. The less she knows the better. I'll tell her we're going down to okapi country for trapping. By God, I hope he's all right. This could queer everything."

"If he is alive we shall find him. Even if he is dead because of the crash we shall find him in the plane. It has been said that this thing will happen, so happen it must."

Winton looked at him curiously, and then for a moment he smiled. "You're entitled to believe that. In a way I'm glad you do, but how you reconcile it with all the other things you know . . . all your European training."

"It is not difficult. Every country has this kind of belief. I have had my fortune told in Paris, in Amsterdam, by sincere people. N'Dene is equally sincere and gifted."

Winton nodded, but his eyes were on the silent set.

"Let's get the men together and go. The hardest and fastest you've got. I'll have a word with Nina as we go by the lake later in the day. Damn and blast it, why did this have to happen at the last moment?"

# CHAPTER TWO

SINCLAIR had been out of the trees about three hours and was now working his way up the open foothills towards the mountains. He'd had enough of trees, days of them, days of the great Congo rain forest which made one feel that one was just going round and round in a steamy glass bottle, getting nowhere.

The sun was dropping fast and he knew that he had little time before darkness. Somewhere, higher up, he hoped to find a cave or shelter of some kind amongst the rocks. It was good to feel the air moving about one, good not to feel that every breath one took was just sucking in a rich rankness that clogged the lungs. In the last four days he had only met two people. They were Abandiya, and he hadn't understood a word they said. But they had taken him to their village and he had spent a night there and then rested a day.

He wanted to be as high as possible before nightfall. The previous night he had had little sleep, keeping awake to mend his fire. He'd lost most of his stuff, including his rifle, days ago in the jeep crash, and a revolver was little comfort at night. Last night had been particularly un-comfortable, twice he'd heard leopards coughing near his camp, and for an hour there had been a crashing and banging about in the near trees as though a lot of crazy removers had been tossing furniture around. He wasn't a man who suffered from nerves or imaginary fears, but he had gone up to the lower fork of a tree above his fire for the hour unashamedly.

The slope began to steepen now, rising to the mountains proper. The straps of his pack bit through his bush shirt and chafed at his shoulders which were wet with sweat.

With every step he took his revolver holster thumped against his hip in a maddening way. He was a bloody fool, of course, to be doing this.

He stopped to light a cigarette which he knew would do nothing for him, his mouth was too dry and the cigarettes were forest damp and battered. As he struck a match he heard a rifle shot. It was so unexpected that he stood there motionless until the match burnt his fingers.

The shot had come from above him and away to his left. He began to climb on towards the spot. A little later there came another shot. Just one that set the rocks echoing. The deliberate spacing of the shots puzzled him. He pulled out his revolver and fired twice. He waited, listening. After a while there were two rifle shots, not quite so closely spaced as his. Sinclair fired two more shots. The rifle answered.

He climbed on, going caterwise along the steep mountain flank now. After about a half a mile the mountainside fell away into a steep gorge-like hanging valley which had been hidden by the slope as he approached. Thrust out over the valley was a high bluff of rocky headland, the strata of the rocks lying horizontally, giving the impression of a gigantic pile of plates. As he came out on to the edge of the rough drop, the rifle spoke from away to his right. He turned and followed the line of the gorge upwards. The boulders had given way now to small cliff-like slabs and loose piles of rubble and earth that fanned away from the foot of the rock faces. As he was crossing one of these he heard a shout.

Looking upwards he saw a low rock face, overhung with a great bank of thorn and piled boulders. He went up the loose, sliding earth to the top of the moraine. Before him was a small-mouthed cave opening. A man in bush shirt, drill trousers, and with a four or five days' growth of beard, sat with his back against one side of the cave opening. Across his knees rested a rifle.

As Sinclair came up to him, he raised a hand and smiled.

"Hi, there."

The smile suddenly turned to a grimace of pain and he dropped his hand to his right side.

"Hi, yourself. What's the trouble?"

Sinclair squatted down alongside him.

"Cracked a few ribs some days ago. Strapped 'em up myself and they seemed to work all right. Until yesterday — then they began to give me hell. Who are you, and what in God's name are you doing on this bit of the map?"

"Sinclair . . . Bill Sinclair. The answer to the other question is longer. And you?"

"Hadlow. Curiously enough, Bill too. Plane crashed in the Ebola six days ago. Been footing it ever since. Not really my kind of travel. I suppose you haven't got any whiskey on you? Oh, Jesus—" he suddenly doubled forward and pressed his hand to his side, and then when his head came up he smiled. "Sorry, it gets me like a mule kick now and then."

Sinclair slipped off his pack and fished in it for his flask. He handed it to Hadlow and said, "Not much left. Finish it. Take your time over it. I'll get a fire going. Soup and my last tin of beef."

"I'm not fussy." Hadlow put the flask to his lips and drank and when he had finished, he sighed. "What wonderful stuff it is. Where are you heading?"

"Bisaka. Know it?"

"No. These parts are off my beat. Flew a couple of crazy journalists from Nairobi across to a place called Bangui. Private charter. My own plane. Why the hell anyone should want to get into the Congo just now, I wouldn't know. Got off track coming back. Hit a storm and had to come down in the river. Only place. Plane's a complete and bloody write-off."

"Well, sit there and take it easy."

Sinclair went out and collected some wood for a fire and then started it just inside the mouth of the cave. The sun, red-eyed from a tiring day, was almost below the mountain crests now. He mixed up a packet of soup in a tin with water from his bottle and stood it on the side embers of the fire. Then he gave Hadlow a hand to rise and walk into the cave. He made the few steps with obvious pain and then lowered himself gingerly to the sandy cave floor, leaning his back against a rock.

"Bloody ribs. All right so long as I don't move."

"You oughtn't to do any more walking with them. I'll leave you here tomorrow and scout around. Must be a village somewhere. Get some natives to make up a litter and carry you."

"Let's see how I feel in the morning."

When they had finished their soup and the warm mess of bully beef, Hadlow said, "You haven't answered the second part of my question. You don't have to. But it's going to be a long night and I'm not ready for sleep."

Sinclair grinned. "It won't take all that long."

He liked this man. He was like himself in more ways than one. Not just in what he did, but in his manner. He took what came and didn't make too much fuss about it. That was the way to be. They were about the same size and build. Near enough the same age, too, he guessed. Nairobi. They could have run into one another any time. Odd they hadn't, really. Nairobi wasn't so far from Entebbe, and they were in the same business.

"You know Uganda Airfreight Limited?"

"Heard of it. Crumby little outfit, isn't it?"

Sinclair laughed. "Yes, I suppose it is. But I worked for them."

"Pilot?" The surprise in the man's voice was frank.

"Yes."

"Well I'll be damned. A couple of stranded birds."

"Not exactly. I'm down for a long time. Had my wings clipped. Two years' suspension of my certificate."

"What happened?"

"It was all a bit tricky. There was a girl, and she preferred me to the chap who ran the show. Stupid, really.

He had far more cash—but she couldn't take his face. So he decided to take it out on me. He needn't have bothered. The girl wasn't the kind who was going to stick to me or anyone long. But he was impatient, I suppose. So he fixed me."

"How?"

"Too easy. He got a pal of his to doctor my drink before I took off. Just an ordinary glass of beer." Sinclair nodded at the empty flask by Hadlow's side. "I can take my share of that stuff with the best of them. But not when I'm flying. Yes, they fixed my beer and timed it nicely for a short trip. It put me in blinkers as I was coming in."

"What a bastard!"

"Crashed—beautifully. No passengers, thank the stars. Just freight and a coloured boy. I came off light but the boy was smacked up a bit. Then the evidence was rigged against me. He went to a lot of careful trouble. Witnesses, the whole lot. Drunk before take-off. Licence suspended two years. The only one who did well out of it was the boy. Broken leg and arm and a nice wad of insurance money. Made his fortune. So"—Sinclair fished into his pocket for his cigarettes, lit one for Hadlow and then one for himself, and went on—"I took off. Here I am, heading for Bisaka. Get a job up there without formalities much, I'm told. I'm not sitting on the ground for two years for anyone."

"I hope you're right about the formalities in Bisaka. That kind of thing follows you around."

"We'll see. Funny we never ran in to one another. Used to go in and out of Nairobi a lot. We were mostly freight."

"I hadn't been there long. Durban's my spot, really. Like you, I keep moving. Looking for a jackpot. But I've never been able to work the oracle—".

He broke off and his head went back against the rock and he laughed. It was a curious little laugh. Then his head came forward and in the firelight Sinclair noticed that his forehead, half hidden by a straggling wing of loose brown hair, was beaded with sweat.

He stood up.

"Time we turned in. You're better off lying flat with those ribs."

Hadlow nodded and Sinclair saw his face twist with a spurt of pain. He went out and got some more wood, gathering it by torchlight, and then came back and made up the fire. He fished his own blankets out of the pack and then a single blanket from Hadlow's roll. He gave him one of his blankets and they stretched out with the fire between them and the mouth of the cave. They lay in silence for a while and then Hadlow said, "What were you in the war?"

"South African Air Force. Finished up in Italy."

"I'd have thought you could have done better than freight jobs. B.O.A.C., for instance."

"Can't stand the routine and the spit and polish. I like something on my own. This bloody world's getting too big, too organised."

"Could be. But not this neck of the woods. The Congo's a pot on the boil and you can't get near the pot for the number of cooks around it. God, what a mess. Still, there's always a profit in trouble for someone. . . . Like to leave your cigarettes and matches handy? I'll be awake for sure with these bloody ribs."

\*     \*     \*

Sinclair woke twice during the night. Once it was to find Hadlow smoking, the red glow of the cigarette lighting up the low rock ceiling as he drew at it. Somewhere far down the slope there was the quick rattle of stones where an animal passed . . . jackal or hyena, the sharp-faced opportunists.

The second time he woke it was to hear Hadlow coughing. The coughing passed quickly and he heard the man sigh and then begin to snore, thick and heavy. He was cold so he got up and mended the fire and then wrapped the single blanket around him. Before he slept he found himself shivering once or twice and he wished there was some whiskey left to take against the cold. Hot days and cold nights and the sweaty dampness of the forest were just the things for malaria. Hoped he wasn't going to get a touch because the touches with him went on too long. He lay there, thinking of the long road behind him from Entebbe. The jeep had been a mistake, of course. He shouldn't have bothered with it . . . Ruwenzori, right up to Mungbere, but there he should have sold it and taken the train to Lienartville. The Congo roads weren't worth a damn. Or he should have hired a boy to take turns with the driving. That had been a moment, waking up at the wheel, knowing he'd dropped off, and seeing the trees coming up at him and just having time to fling himself out before it went over. Right over the edge of the gorge it had gone, like a bat out of hell, and smack into the river. And after a two hours' climb down all he had been able to salvage was the pack and a few odds and ends of provisions. His valise and the jeep were gone . . . passport, papers, the whole bloody issue.

So what did you do? If you couldn't fly, you rode, and if you couldn't ride, you walked . . . over the Uele and over the Uere, heading north for Bisaka.

As he dropped off to sleep he heard Hadlow begin to cough again.

When he woke the sun was just coming up turning the dew on the rock faces into a blaze of diamond hard brilliance. He went out, got more wood for the fire and set it going. Then he rinsed out a tin with a little water from his bottle—what a bastard it was losing all his equipment —and put it on the fire for coffee. When the water began to boil he went into the cave to wake Hadlow.

The man was lying on his side, the blankets rolled away from his shoulders. Sinclair shook him but Hadlow made no response. Then, where the man's face lay against the side of his half empty pack which he had used as a pillow, he saw the pack and the sand beneath it stained with blood. He turned the man over and with the movement he knew that there was no life in the body. Hadlow's face stared up at him, eyes open, and around his mouth and over his right cheek was the rusty-coloured dried blood of the sudden haemorrhage that had killed him.

Sinclair stood there looking down at him. Then he put his hand to the man's eyes and smoothed down the lids. He pulled the blanket up over his face and went back to the fire. He lifted the tin of coffee from the embers, wrapping his neckscarf round the hot metal to hold it, and went and sat on a rock outside the cave.

He was shocked. Not by death, for he had seen that often enough. But by a curious sense of loss. Poor bloody Hadlow. He'd liked him. They would have got on well together. And now he was gone. All that coughing in the night . . .

He sat there, sipping at his coffee, and it was a long time before he could bring himself to do anything. He sat at the cave mouth with the dead man behind him and watched the new day strike down at the mountain slopes. Far away a slow curl of mist began to lift from the endless, south-stretching mat of green forest trees.

Finally he went back into the cave. Hadlow wore a canvas wind-breaker over his shirt. Sinclair emptied the pockets of the wind-breaker and the trousers. Farther back in the cave the floor was loose sand. With a large flat piece of stone he scraped away at the sand and made a shallow grave and then went back and dragged Hadlow to it. Hadlow's face was set in death with a curious, unsurprised, non-committal expression, a worn, experienced face. He put his handkerchief over it and began to scrape back the sand. When the sand was in place he collected rocks from outside and piled them over the mound. He made a good job of it, sweating with the labour. He didn't want any damned hyenas to dig him out. As he put the last rock in place he felt a surge of quick giddiness through his head. He stood there and swore softly to himself. He was in for a bout of malaria. Even the hot coffee hadn't warmed him up from the night. In an hour it would be punching at him. He picked up his cigarettes and matches where they had rested by Hadlow's sleeping place and went outside to sort out the stuff he had taken from the man. Already he knew that he wasn't going to stay.

Hadlow had a rifle and a bandolier half-full of ammunition. Well, he'd take that. He had nothing to get game for himself. In the man's pack were a couple of shirts, some socks, the usual stuff for washing and a crumpled map of the Belgian Congo. From his pockets he had taken a half-used cheque book from a Durban bank; a wallet with a mixture of American, English and South African notes, about seventy pounds in all, a Durban club membership card, driving licence and a dog-eared photograph of a girl on a beach in a bikini; a passport, British, and loose from his pockets a bunch of keys, a cigarette lighter, a small pocket compass, and that was all.

He opened the passport. A slip of paper fell from it. It was Hadlow's licence for private and commercial flying. The passport itself was battered and stained. Mr William Garner Hadlow. The details on the second page listed him as an *Engineer*, born at Birmingham on the 2nd of June, 1931. Height five feet ten and a half inches; hair brown, and special peculiarities—*Nil*.

The photograph was stained and worn and might have been anyone with hair on the head, and the passport had been renewed by the British Consul at Durban a year before. Sinclair put all the stuff away into his own pack. The rifle was a S.M.L.E. ·303, a rebuilt job from the No. 4 rifle of World War II. It was a good feeling to have a gun in his hands again. It meant he could eat.

Once he started moving, although he knew by now that he was in for a bout of malaria, the exercise held it back.

He took things easy the whole of that day, working his way north along the line of the mountains. Late in the afternoon he shot a duiker and he made camp almost where he had killed it, building a fire and broiling some of the flesh over the red embers. And then he slept, or tried to sleep, sitting up with his back against a rock, wrapped in two blankets and shivering, his mind floating off often into a feverish delirium. In his moments of clearness, he knew that he was in for a very bad bout. He hadn't had such a fever for two years.

The next morning he forced himself to get going again, knowing he must find a native homestead, find somewhere where he could lie under cover and let the fever take its course. He staggered along the line of the hills for hours, resting, then forcing himself on, talking nonsense to himself and shivering under the burning sun. Time lost all meaning for him. He was aware of the hills curving away slowly to the west and he crossed them by a low saddle and saw the green of trees far below him. He went stumbling downwards. Then suddenly his feet slipped from under him and he fell and rolled, and then just let himself roll, no strength in him to resist. When he came to rest he just lay there, sweat misting his eyes and the taste of dirt in his dry mouth.

He drifted off into sleep. Once he thought he heard someone talking to him. Then words came more clearly to him. Strange words which he could not understand. He opened his eyes wearily and briefly. There was a face above him, a dark native face with a big flat nose, thick lips . . . an old face, full of wrinkles and topped with a mop of whitish hair. Sinclair smiled, tried to say something and heard the parched croak that came from his own mouth. A boy's face, shining chocolate-coloured, appeared at the man's side and a pair of dark, wondering eyes looked down at him.

# CHAPTER THREE

A LITTLE way up the hill behind his hut N'Dene had a small patch of ground where he grew his herbs and medicine plants. N'Dene, like any good witch-doctor among the Azande, was also a master of leechcraft. The Azande regard most sicknesses as the result of witchcraft or sorcery except in the instance of newly born children whose souls are so new that they cannot be expected to attract evil and who, anyway, are so newly arrived in the world that they are free to depart with ease. Around his little plot N'Dene had put long lengths of a magical creeper supported on small sticks, for this creeper was well known to be able to break the spell of anyone wishing evil to the small garden.

Many things like these N'Dene was teaching his small grandson, his favourite. When they went for a walk together up to the termite mounds or along the shores of the lake, N'Dene, the child's hand in his, would talk away. He would point out the magical creeper *gire* for protecting gardens and which could also be wound round the wrist as a charm, or he would point out the ripe fruit of the *vuruma*, round and full of sap like a woman's breast, whose juice is given to a nursing mother when her milk fails. When the homestead had been built at this end of the lake a year before and the *tuka*, the ghost shrine, had been erected before the hut, he had taken the boy into the forest and searched out the thin, spike-leafed *rangu ambiri* and planted it at the foot of the shrine and N'Dene had said, 'You are rangu ambiri, may no leopard come into this place. May no wild beast come to eat the fowls, our dogs or our people.' With the child N'Dene was always happy, even though he knew that not always did the boy listen, but he was happy because he knew that unless the old men like himself talked and the young listened then nothing could be known and remembered and passed on.

N'Dene was in his hut now with the child and with the white man they had found sick on the hills. The white man was in a fever, not knowing them, not knowing where he was, and for a day N'Dene had been doctoring him with the juice of his medicine plants. But N'Dene knew that his medicine was not strong enough now to fight the witchcraft of the fever.

"Someone," he was telling the boy, "has made a strong bad magic against this man. But there is no bad magic which cannot be driven out. We must take the evil from him."

The boy, round-eyed, watched as N'Dene took his sharp hunting knife and at the side of the man's left temple made two small cuts in the skin. The blood beaded the lines of the cut. N'Dene then took a hollow gazelle's horn which had a hole through the narrow end. He slipped into his mouth a small lump of beeswax, pouching it like a monkey, and then put the wide open end of the horn on the temple incisions. He sucked hard, creating a vacuum in the horn and then, when he felt the taste of blood on his tongue, he rolled the beeswax lump to the end of the horn and bit on it, sealing the small hole. He stood, holding the horn against the temple while the vacuum, sealed by the wax, drew the blood from the man's body, drew the blood and with it the evil of the fever. When he judged that the horn was full he called to the boy for a small wooden bowl. With the end of his knife he pierced the wax and held the bowl under the horn so that the blood dripped into it. When the dripping ceased he took the horn away from Sinclair's temple. Using some of the blood to help him make a paste, he put *botoli* plant leaves in the bowl, pounded them up and then spread the plaster over the two cuts.

Sinclair groaned a little, opened his eyes and stared at N'Dene. Then his eyes closed.

N'Dene said to the boy, "By tomorrow he will be well." He handed the bowl to the boy. "Take this down to the lake and clean it well."

The boy went out and N'Dene followed him and he squatted down in the shade of the thatched roof overhang and watched the boy make his way down to the lake, disappearing through the trees.

Half an hour later the boy came back through the trees and N'Dene saw that with him was the daughter of Major Winton from the camp at the far end of the lake. With her also was one of the boys from her camp. He watched her coming up towards him and he was glad to see her. Her father gave work to many of his people. But he liked her for herself, not because she was Major Winton's daughter. In fact, there was no blood of Major Winton in her. Mabenge had told him this, that her true father was dead and Major Winton had taken her mother, now also dead, in marriage when this white girl had been twelve or thirteen years old.

She came up to him, bare-headed, the sun bright on her pale hair and about her neck was the flash of a red scarf. N'Dene liked the way she walked, long and free and smooth, without effort, like a gazelle. But it was wrong that she should wear trousers and shirt like a man, and carry a rifle like a man. A woman should be a woman. He rose as she came close to him and bowed his head.

"Greetings."

"Greetings, N'Dene." She smiled and held out a small tin of tobacco as a gift. He took it without comment, but he knew that before she went he must also give her a present and he knew what would please her most. He and the boy had found a young golden crane by the lake side some days ago. One of its legs had been broken. When the boy had wanted to kill it N'Dene had stopped him. He had no magic to heal broken bones. In his race only the members of the Amozungu clan could be bone-setters. The great M'Bori had decided this in the far Beginning when one of the clan had begat a child without arms or legs. M'Bori had told the father in a dream to burn the child and mix his ashes with oil and to use the ointment to heal broken limbs and even to this day only the Amozungu clan could set bones. But with the white people there was a different medicine magic, good only in their hands, and this girl could take a broken animal or bird and heal it. Her camp was full of them, for she and her father had a great love of animals. For her, the crane would be a great gift. He could picture now the smile that would come over her face when he handed her the wicker cage in which the bird crouched.

Speaking his own language, the girl said, "You have a white man here, N'Dene."

N'Dene nodded. "He was lying on the hills in a fever. By tomorrow he will be awake and begin to be well. I have taken the fever sorcery from his blood."

"Then tomorrow I will come with some boys and carry him to our camp. Can I see him?"

N'Dene stood aside for her to enter the hut, but he did not go inside with her. He squatted down again in the shade and the small boy sat at his side and began to prepare his pipe. The boy who had come up from the camp with the white woman said, "In two days time, O N'Dene, we make a trap for leopards on the far side of the lake. Will you come and make *bingiya* medicine for good hunting?"

N'Dene, who knew the man well and his reputation, grunted and spoke severely for it was not good to talk of magic when a white woman paid him a visit. "It is not for hunting you need the *bingiya* medicine. You would steal some of it and use it for hunting women. I know you, wart-hog."

After a time the white girl came out of the hut and

N'Dene got to his feet, whispering to the boy to go and get the crane.

"He is sick, N'Dene. You are sure he will be better to-morrow?"

"Tomorrow he will be better. You spoke to him?"

"Yes, but he does not hear me. But I have looked through his things, N'Dene. He is an Englishman called William Hadlow. I will come tomorrow for him."

N'Dene nodded. The boy came round the hut with the crane in its wicker basket. N'Dene took it and handed it to her, and he saw her face light up as she raised it and put her hand between the bars to touch the bird.

"Its leg is broken, but you have medicine to mend it."

"Yes, N'Dene, I have medicine."

As she went away with her boy, down towards the lake shore, N'Dene watched her go, sucking at his pipe. Although he liked her, there were many things about her which he had to regret. She was a woman and women were of little importance except for child bearing and working. This girl had medicine witchcraft, and she hunted and dressed like a man, and he knew that she could travel hard and fast like a man, and yet she was a woman. Once he and his grandson in their canoe had seen her bathing naked from one of the lake islands, stand-ing tall and slim and with high round breasts. For him-self, an old man, and the boy so young, there had been no shame in the sight of her sun-tanned body. But a woman was a woman, no matter her colour, to young men, and he had spoken to Major Winton about it and when he had seen her bathing again she had worn a covering.

\*    \*    \*

By next morning Sinclair's fever was gone. He awoke, clear-headed, but feeling weak and hungry. When N'Dene came in to him it was hard for them to speak to-gether for Sinclair had no Zande, but years and years ago when N'Dene had been a young man he had worked for a

brief time in a Catholic Mission and had picked up a few
words of French which still clung to him. He brought
Sinclair food and some eleusine beer and then water to
wash and while he did so he explained how he had found
him and brought him down from the hills.

Bisaka, he explained, was about four days away on foot.
But Sinclair wouldn't be able to travel rough for some
days yet. There was something about 'the white major's
daughter' which Sinclair couldn't make out, but he did
get that there was a European camp of some kind at the far
end of the lake which he could see through the hut door.

After he had eaten and washed he went and sat outside
and N'Dene presented his three wives to him and the
various other members of the homestead.

Sinclair liked the old man and he could see that he was
treated with enormous respect by the other members of
the household.

About midday, when he had returned to the hut to
escape the fierce heat and was lying on his blankets on the
floor, the bright frame of sunlight at the door was darkened
and a girl came into the hut. He had been half-dozing and
had been vaguely aware of N'Dene talking to someone outside. She came over to him and when, still a little fuddled
with the heat and half-asleep, he made to rise she shook
her head at him.

"Don't try to get up, Mr. Hadlow. I just looked in to
see if you were fit enough to make the trip to our camp."

Sinclair sat up, and before he could say anything she
went on, "I'm Nina Winton. My step-father has a camp
at the far end of the lake. I didn't hear until yesterday
that you were here and then it was too late for me to do
anything. N'Dene had taken you in hand." She laughed
and it was a bright, cheerful sound in the darkened hut.
"Probably pumped you full of weird potions and muttered
spells over you—but they seem to have worked."

"I don't know what he did, but I'm certainly better
and grateful to him. But look, don't call me Hadlow."

"Well, of course not, if you don't want me to. What do they call you? Bill, for short?"

"Well, I'm Bill, yes. But how did you know?"

She laughed again. "I should apologise I suppose. But when I came up yesterday I went through your stuff and saw your passport. It wasn't just curiosity. It's just that a white man turning up like you did . . . well, one just wants to know who he is. How do you feel about moving?"

Sinclair smiled. "Well, I don't know. I haven't really tried the motor out yet."

"We could have you carried down." She seated herself on one of N'Dene's small wooden stools and brought out matches and cigarettes. "I don't smoke myself, but I brought these up. I noticed yesterday that you hadn't any in your pack."

"Well, thank you. You're very observant—and kind. I should have malaria more often if I get this sort of attention."

He lit a cigarette, feeling the amusement in himself at the way this girl had walked in and established herself without any fuss, with an easy friendship—and getting his name wrong.

"How far is your place?"

"About five miles down the lake."

"Then I think I'll rest up here for the day. I can get down there on my own feet tomorrow. I'm heading for Bisaka."

"Bisaka? Then you're lucky. There's a twice monthly plane comes out to us with stores from there. It's due in three days. You could wait for that. It's a four or five day trek to Bisaka anyway."

"It sounds a good idea. What are you doing out in the wilds like this?"

"My father makes animal films and collects for zoos. We've been here about six months . . . at least I have. He's known this place for years and been here many times."

She stood up, smiling. "They always say make the first visit to an invalid a short one. I brought you another present as well. Some tinned stuff in case you don't go for Azande food . . . you know, fried termites and ground nuts. I've left it with N'Dene. I had an idea that you wouldn't fancy being bumped about in a litter for five miles."

"Frankly no. But you don't have to go. Tell me, what's Bisaka like?"

"The end of nowhere. You've got friends there?"

"No. I'm looking for a job. There's a small air transport company there. I'm a pilot."

"I should have thought you'd have flown there rather than walking."

"I set out in a jeep but it got smashed up. Before Lienartville. I was going to fly from there, but somehow the plan went wrong and then I got lost. Also, I ought to put you right. You see—"

N'Dene's head came round the hut opening and he spoke rapidly to Nina in her own tongue. When he had finished she turned to Sinclair and said, "Sorry, I've got to go. One of my boys has just arrived to say he's found a python in one of our animal pits."

"Python! You mean you tackle pythons?"

She smiled. "They're all right if you get four or five men on them and keep the kinks out of them. Oh," she turned on the way to the door, "I put a bottle of whiskey in with the food. See you tomorrow."

She was gone before he could say anything.

He lay back on his blankets and finished the cigarette slowly. It would have been easy to imagine that he still had malaria and had dreamt the whole thing. She had been in and out before he could really get down to sorting things out. What a girl. First she got his name wrong. Then she was really on the ball about cigarettes and whiskey. He smiled to himself. She just hadn't given him a chance to tell her his real name.

The mistake was reasonable enough. Hadlow's was the only passport he had. His own was at the bottom of a river. Until this moment he hadn't given any great thought to the consequences of his lost passport. Once in Bisaka he would have to apply for another. The formalities involved in doing this could easily end in his recent history being revealed. Then there would be no flying job for him. The answer was obvious. Hadlow's passport was a godsend. He just took over the man's identity and his papers. Why not? There were no snags in it so far as he could see. So long as you had papers there was a magic in them for all authority. You existed. Without them you became an object of enquiry. And in a new republic the authorities could be very officious sometimes. Bisaka wasn't in the Congo Republic. It was on the other side of the Bomu river, in what had once been French Equatorial Africa, the old province of Ubangi-Shari. Now it was a new republic, the Central Africa Republic, a member of the French Community. In a place like that it would be wise to steer clear of too many official contacts. All he had to do to avoid his past history coming up in Bisaka was to take Hadlow's name.

It was taking a chance, but he wasn't the kind of man to worry about that. If the worse came to the worse he could just admit the deception, take a dressing down from the authorities in Bisaka, even a fine or a few weeks in prison, and then move on. At the best, he could have two years under another name and be able to fly. That was the great point. He could go on flying with a legitimate certificate. Bill Sinclair. Bill Hadlow. Hadlow wouldn't have cared a damn—would have done the same thing himself. No one in Bisaka was likely to have heard of the real Hadlow. Durban was his place and these parts strange to him.

He lay there thinking about it. It would certainly avoid awkward questions from some official making a bad-tempered display of authority. He could walk into Bisaka

with a new identity. The battered photograph in the passport could be anyone. They were about the same height,
and his hair was brown, a little lighter in colour maybe
than Hadlow's, but brown.

Outside came the sound of women's and children's voices
as N'Dene's people came back from their work in the little
cultivated plots near the lake. Sinclair reached for another
cigarette. The girl had really been responsible. Good for
her.

He remembered her standing in the shadow-hung hut,
smiling, a good-looking, tall girl with everything in the
right place, and talking easily as though she'd known him
for years. If he got a flying job the lake wasn't far from
Bisaka. . . . He could drop in and see her from time to
time. Maybe she even came into Bisaka. A good-looking
girl who obviously knew how to handle herself . . . and
how to look after herself, too. He smiled to himself.
Pythons gave her no trouble. No doubt men didn't either.

*     *     *

Sinclair made the trip to the Wintons' camp the next
morning. N'Dene and his grandson went with him, carrying his pack and his rifle until they were about half a mile
from the camp. Here N'Dene and the boy left him and
turned back. Sinclair made N'Dene a present of what
was left of the cigarettes that Nina had brought, his pocket
knife, and a cheap metal can-opener. The opener had a
little hole in its handle and N'Dene was delighted with it.
He would wear it round his neck with his magic whistle
and other charms. It meant nothing to him that the
opener was inscribed — *Property of the Gaillard Hotel,
Entebbe.*

Sinclair had enjoyed the walk down the lake. It lay in
a long curving crescent, flanked by mountains. To the
north the ground rose to a low pass. On this the west side
of the lake a wide mud and sand packed beach spread
back from the waters, making a perfect runway for three or

four miles. Nearer the camp, which was at the north end
of the lake, the water was studded with small islands and
the low, warty mounds of flamingo nests near the far
shore. Now and again a handful of birds got up and
winged rapidly along the lake, keeping low over the water
and then coming down with an awkward landing to feed
in the shallows. The water was full of duck and cranes.
The heat from the sun-baked beach came up into Sinclair's face as though someone had left an oven door open.

Near the end of the run of beach a bluff of high ground
ran out into the lake, its foot fringed with tall reeds through
which a wide path had been cut. He went through this
and came out on to a small beach. At its far end a clump
of trees marked the foot of a low cliff. In their shade he
saw a collection of tents and two or three reed-thatched
open shelters. As he got closer he saw that two of the open
huts were full of rough animal cages. Under the third hut
was a long wooden table and a couple of young Rhesus
monkeys sat on the thatch and watched him approach.
Up the small cliff side he could see two or three native
boys cutting brushwood. As he came up to the hut a baby
gazelle, tottery on thin legs, rose from the shade of the
table and came towards him, thrusting its nose into the
palm of his hand and then turning and trotting at his side
back to the hut.

Sinclair went in under the shade and dumped his pack
and rifle on the rough table. On the table was a book, a
pair of binoculars and a shot gun. One of the monkeys
hung its head below the edge of the thatch and chattered
at him.

From away to his right a voice called suddenly, "Hullo,
there."

He turned and faced the lake. Nina Winton was swimming lazily towards the shore. She came out of the lake
and walked up towards him, the water dripping from her
white bathing suit. When she was close to him she raised
her hands taking her loose hair and squeezing it free of

water. Then she took a towel from one of the roof sup-
ports and began to dry her arms and legs.

He was amused at the way she had come out of the lake
and accepted his presence. No awkwardness, no polite
phrases . . . here he was and that was it. He said, "It
looks pretty good in there. Maybe I should try it."

She shook her head. "Not today. You've only just got
over malaria. Tomorrow."

"Yes, nurse."

Towelling herself still, she went on, "We're lucky with
the lake. No crocodiles. No *bilharzia*. The major
wouldn't let me go in otherwise."

"The major? Your father?"

"Step-father." She said it casually. She straightened up
from towelling her legs, and added, "My real father died
years ago. Now then, I'll get you some beer, and after
that we'll get you fixed up. How are you feeling?"

"Fine. A bit slow on the old legs. But by tomorrow I
shall be in shape."

She disappeared into one of the tents. When she came
back, carrying some tins of beer and glasses, she was
dressed . . . a tall, slim, cool-looking girl wearing a white
shirt tucked into the top of white linen slacks. Almost a
Riviera get-up Sinclair thought, and he wondered whether
she had abandoned khaki drill in honour of her guest.
Could be. When there was a man around a woman did
these things instinctively.

Sinclair spent two nights at the lake camp and he got to
know a lot about Nina Winton. Although she had gone
to school in England, she had spent a great deal of her
time in Africa, one place and another. Her real father had
been a Professor of Sociology at the Cairo Egyptian
University. He had died when she was twelve and her
mother had married again. She did not talk much about
her step-father and Sinclair felt that she hadn't really
accepted him as another father. She admired him, talked
a great deal about his work, but there was no touch of

affection in her voice when he was mentioned. After she had left school she had worked as the private secretary of a research lecturer in African Sociology at Oxford—an old friend of her father's. But she clearly had not cared for secretarial work and six months ago had come out to join her step-father. In those months she had learned a great deal of the Azande language and had obviously become very useful to Major Winton. She had a great love of animals, and a way with them. She supervised the care and feeding of the collection, and the place was swarming with invalid animals and pets. Once every three months a consignment was taken down to Bisaka by plane and then flown on through Khartoum and Cairo to their various destinations. In addition she helped in the various filming projects which her step-father carried out in the country around the lake.

On their second evening, after dinner, they took a stroll along the beach. There was a thin slip of moon and as they came back through the path cut in the reeds Sinclair took her arm to help her over the tricky ground. Out on the beach he kept his hand on her arm still. Back at the hut they sat together and had a whiskey night-cap watching the silver-jagged moon reflections over the water.

Sinclair said, "You like this kind of life? Stuck away in Africa?"

"Yes. For six months, or a year. I love it. But I like the other, too. The bright lights, dancing and music. Don't you?"

"Yes. But I'm a working man. I go where the jobs are."

"But why Bisaka? I should have thought a pilot could get a job well . . . somewhere else, somewhere more civilised."

Sinclair grinned. "Sometimes a chap wants to tuck himself away somewhere for a spell. Anyway, I don't like the plushy sort of jobs. B.O.A.C. and that kind. You can make more money in the smaller, less fussy outfits."

She looked at him but said nothing and he wondered

how much she was reading into the evasion. Enough, probably. She didn't have to have things spelled out in black and white. Neither did she ask awkward questions when obviously they weren't going to be welcome.

When their whiskey was finished he walked with her to the tents. They stopped outside hers and she turned to him.

"Tomorrow, I'll get you up early. We can go out on the lake and see the early morning flight of the flamingoes and then have a bathe from one of the islands. The Bisaka plane will be here at midday. It only stays a couple of hours."

"If I get a job in Bisaka, I'll be back."

She smiled. "I'm sure you will."

For a moment Sinclair was taken by surprise then he laughed lightly.

"You're a thought reader as well as everything else."

"No, I mean . . . well it would be nice if you did come back."

"You mean that?"

"Of course."

He put up his hands and took her by the shoulders. Her eyes which were bright blue in daylight, were dark and deep now and under the moonlight her hair seemed paler, moon-bleached. He drew her to him and he kissed her and as his arms slipped round her she kissed him back. After a moment they separated and he looked at her, the small smile about his lips matching hers.

"I've wanted to do that for some time. But I wasn't quite sure how it would be received by a python-handling girl."

She laughed gently. "You wouldn't have done it unless I wanted it too. If I like a man enough. . . . You know, that little bit more, then I like to be kissed. It's natural, isn't it?"

"If you say so. That goes for me too."

He drew her to him and this time the kiss was longer

and above his own pleasure, he could feel her pleasure, frank and open and generous, and beyond this he could sense a growing feeling that somewhere along the line she was handling things and not him. It was a new sensation.

When they parted, she said, "You needn't worry about the python. These boys always exaggerate. It was only about six feet long. Good night, Bill."

She was gone into her tent before he could say anything.

*     *     *

The next morning she woke him before sunrise with a cup of coffee. When he was dressed and shaved he went down to the lakeside where she was operating a foot pump, topping up the air in a large R.A.F. sea rescue dinghy. He took over the chore from her.

"It's got a leak somewhere, so we'd better take the pump."

As they got into the clumsy craft one of the tame Rhesus monkeys came bounding down the beach and leapt into the dinghy.

"What's this," asked Sinclair. "A cabin boy?"

Nina laughed. "That's Angus—he's mad about boats. Even this crazy thing."

The monkey settled on her shoulder undisturbed by her work with the paddle and they headed out over the lake, both of them idling the dinghy along. There was little room in it and Nina sat ahead of Sinclair, her back resting against his knees. For so early in the morning she was bright and full of talk and Sinclair who was a slow morning starter was content to listen to her. She had that gift of never being at a loss for a subject and of never boring.

Her father was still in the process of making a film about the flamingo colony, a film that would show their life through a complete year-cycle. To the Azande, she explained, the flamingoes were totem birds, and the one black flamingo—which she said was a melanic aberration —was of special significance. So long as there was a black flamingo leader on the lake everything would go well with the Azande.

"What's melanic?"

She laughed. "I suppose that's too much to expect an uneducated pilot to know."

He leaned forward and kissed her on the nape of her neck.

"It's a darkness of colour resulting from an abnormal development of black pigment in the skin or the hair. That's the dictionary. Just a freak. But the Azande say that so long as there is a black flamingo, then one day their nation will be great again. Sometime, when you come again, I'll tell you about the Azande. The major believes they are the finest race in Africa . . ." Her voice trailed off, and she was silent, the morning broken only by the sound of the dipping of their paddles.

The morning mist was lifting rapidly as the unseen sun behind the eastern mountains began its long climb. High up, a thin ribbon of clouds were touched with an edging of pale gold. A fishing cormorant surfaced close to the dinghy, raised a bone grey beak in surprise at their presence and flipped under indignantly as Angus chattered angrily at it.

Over her shoulder Nina said, "Who's the girl?"

Sinclair did not know what she was talking about and before he could say anything, Nina went on—

"Sorry. But I've been itching with curiosity. Forget I asked it."

"What girl?"

"The one in your wallet. I went through all your stuff when you were ill. It was a terribly tattered photograph."

He was with her then, and he laughed, thinking quickly. He'd almost forgotten that he was supposed to be Hadlow.

"Just a girl. I was very fond of her once. But she upped and married. I only clean out my wallet once every three or four years."

"I thought it might be your wife."

"You know you didn't. Do I look married, or act married?"

"I don't know how you look. Just nice, I think." She screwed her head round and made a face at him.

"Maybe, I should ask the major for a job about the camp. Bisaka seems a long way to go."

For a moment he thought she was going to say something. Then she bent forward and began to put more force into her paddle stroke.

They landed on the largest of the little group of islands and pulled the dinghy a few yards up the sandy beach. Then they walked through the fringe of mango trees up to a small grassy plateau where they could see the lake spread below them, and from here they saw the morning flight of flamingoes go up as the sun's rays touched the water, firing the surface to colour. It was a wonderful spectacle and they stood in silence as the birds wheeled in a great cloud above them, led by the black flamingo.

Sinclair, who did not regard himself as a poetic kind of person, was moved by the sight. This curving lake held in its long mountain trough seemed an enchanted place and for a while it was possible to forget the ceaseless killing and hunting that went on in the forests and great plains, the vast unmethodical cruelty of Nature working without compassion, slaying and maiming and creating in order to slay again. . . . For a while this place seemed a paradise, full of colour, the pink and white birds a gigantic moving fresco above them, the flash of hoopoes and jays among the trees and the lightning streaks of kingfishers searing briefly above the sun-touched waters which were free of crocodile. Sinclair found himself standing with his arm around Nina's shoulder, completely relaxed and aware of a simple happiness within him.

"It's wonderful, isn't it?"

He nodded.

She looked at him, smiled and then pointed towards the far end of the lake. "Look, there's the old fish-hawk.

Every morning when the flamingoes come down he appears, ready to begin work."

High in the northern sky, black against the sunlight, a fish-hawk hovered. Just for a moment Sinclair resented the bird. He was in business, the old, old business; the lion that waited for the buck to come to the water to drink, the otter that slid down into the green depths, stringing a chain of bubbles behind him as he twisted and took the trout, the snake that eased itself like a moving branch to the lip of the nest to take eggs or fledglings . . . they were all in business.

A few minutes later they were swimming in the lake. Nina had worn her swim-suit under her dress and she had brought a pair of the major's trunks for Sinclair. They swam well out from the island, leaving Angus chattering angrily on the shore. Sinclair watched her as she rolled over in the water, her brown shoulders shining, the pale hair streaming and there was something about her complete naturalness which he had never met in any other woman before. All the women he had known seemed to be acting for some purpose. You thought you knew where you were with them all right, but it never seemed to add up to anything real. But this girl was different. She just went on serenely being herself and untroubled by any thought of how she might be impressing other people.

She trod water now, putting a hand on his shoulder and said, "I used to bathe out here naked. It's the only way. But old N'Dene saw me." She laughed. "He turned himself into a Watch Committee and made a protest to the major. The young miss should not bathe without clothing, it would inflame the passions of his young men . . . so the major, who didn't care a damn, issued an order."

Sinclair turned her round, facing her in the water and held her by the shoulders. For all he could see of her now, she might be naked and just looking at her he suddenly felt as though he had gone hollow. To his surprise he heard himself say, "Nina, do you like me?" Before she could answer he remembered that the same sentence with a different name had been his first moment of awkward romance as a boy of sixteen with a schoolgirl. And the response from Nina was the same as it had been then. She just looked at him and nodded, but with none of the other girl's shy confusion.

"Of course I do. Come on, I'll race you back."

She slipped from him and headed for the island and he went after her.

They dried themselves and lay out on the sand in the sun. She let her head rest on his arm and he bent over and kissed her and the hollowness in his stomach was filled with red-hot coals. But as they still kissed and his hands moved on her body she rolled away from him and lay, looking up at his face.

"No?"

She shook her head. "No."

"Why not?"

"Because I want to, and if one wants to, then everything must be right and mustn't be hurried. Men don't care do they, I mean about a sandy beach and Angus looking on like another N'Dene. . . . Oh, Bill, don't look so miserable."

"Am I?"

"Yes."

"You know, I don't get you. You like me. How easy do you find it to like people?"

She laughed again then. "You put it nicely, Bill. But I wouldn't have minded if you'd been blunter. How often do I let men make love to me? Is that it?"

"Forget it."

"No. It's a reasonable question. I let you kiss me and hold me. A girl shouldn't do that to a man just to tease him. And I haven't. But I don't do it often. Very seldom, because one doesn't often meet people one likes. I like you very much, Bill. But not on a sandy beach with the flies biting."

Sinclair reached for his cigarettes. Smoking he looked down at her and let one hand rest on the smooth, warm slope of her shoulder. "I thought I knew most of the answers. But you fox me. Maybe it's because I'm not used to such frankness—"

She laughed, sat up and put her arms around his neck and kissed him quickly.

"Let's go back and have some breakfast."

He stood up and reached down for her hand. She came up and he held her close to him.

"You're a devil. But don't forget Bisaka isn't very far away. I'll be back."

For a moment her face clouded. "The major doesn't like people dropping in here. He says the planes disturb the birds and animals."

"What nonsense.'.

"Yes. But he's very obstinate about what he wants. Anyway, I come into Bisaka sometimes for a day or so."

They stood looking at one another, and then, his hand holding hers, she turned away towards the dinghy and he followed.

# CHAPTER FOUR

THE plane came in late that afternoon. Sinclair saw it clear the mountains to the south of the lake and then dip towards the long run of beach. As it lost height the great lake bowl was filled with the noise of its engines and he saw some of the flamingoes go up, startled from the water, and wing away haphazardly. Watching the plane coming down, Sinclair had a moment of sharp regret that it was to take him away from the lake and Nina. He wasn't given to highly coloured romantic thoughts; but he had been happy here in a simple way, and he acknowledged the enchantment of the place. And, apart from his personal feelings for Nina, he was impressed by her. She worked as hard as any of the coloured boys with the animals, and, no matter what she did, there was a competence and adroitness about her which, he could see, must make her invaluable to Winton in his filming work. He was sorry he was going to miss seeing Winton. He had a curiosity to see this man whom Nina always referred to as 'the major'.

The plane was a D.H. 104 Dove. Sinclair knew them. Two 305 h.p. D.H. Gypsy Queen engines. The landing was a little ragged.

The pilot was a South African, called Pete Laver. He was a man of about thirty, plumpish, fair-haired, with an easy smile and breath that smelled of whiskey. He talked a lot and Sinclair got the impression that he was gently tight. It made him wonder about the air-transport company in Bisaka. Maybe it was a refuge for pilots in trouble. . . .

Laver accepted Sinclair's presence without any great surprise and while the stores were being unloaded by the boys, the three of them sat under the awning and had beer.

When Sinclair went into the tent he had been using to get his pack and rifle, Nina followed him in. He put his arms around her and kissed her. It was as if they had known each other a long time and there was no room for any misunderstanding between them, and no need for a lot of unnecessary words.

Laver took off competently and, in the air, Sinclair soon saw that he knew his business. On the way back to Bisaka Sinclair asked him what he thought were the chances of getting a job. He said, "Shouldn't be difficult. Voyadis— that's the boss—has room for another man. But you must be hard pressed to come up here."

"That's roughly the idea."

"Good enough." Laver turned and winked, and did not pursue the subject. Instead, he went on, "How did you make out with the girl?"

"Nina?"

"Yes. Her step-father's a bit of a bastard, I think. But she's all right. Not my type . . . too damned healthy and all those bloody animals around. But I like her. There's the river."

Below them the great stretch of trees was broken by the wide, lazy sprawl of the Bomu. On the north bank, which was Central Africa Republic territory, the forest ran in a wide belt for about three miles and then broke as the land rose, running away into an ochre haze of sandy, grassy plateau. Southwards was the endless sweep of the great rain forest losing itself in a green, misty haze.

The trip took them about an hour and before Laver went in to land, he circled the plane over Bisaka so that Sinclair could get a look at it.

"It's a dump," Laver said. "But it's home."

Bisaka lay on the inner loop of the river, a sprawl of bungalows and tin shanties with a dust road running down to the riverside where there was a wooden wharf with a

couple of large, corrugated-iron roofed storehouses. They
were over the place too quickly for Sinclair to get much
detail, but he could see that Bisaka was like a hundred
other small African towns he had known. It would be
sun-bitten and dusty and at night there would be the river-
damp and the mosquitoes. Whatever Laver might say, no
one would ever think of it as home. The prospect of two
years in such a dump made Sinclair feel grim, until he
remembered Nina . . . but even she was nearly a hundred
miles away now and what would his chances be of getting
to see her? That was the damned trouble with Africa. It
was just too bloody big.

The airstrip was about a mile from the town and had
been bulldozed out of the forest. At the western end was a
wooden hut, thatched with reed. Above it a wind-sock
hung limply on a pole. Behind the hut were two large
corrugated iron hangars, open-fronted, and what looked
like a petrol dump covered with tarpaulins.

Laver came in with a couple of big bumps that made
Sinclair wince, and then taxied up to the hut. There was
no one about except a coloured mechanic, an oldish man
in dirty white overalls, and no sign of any other plane
except an Auster Aiglet which stood outside one of the
hangars.

Laver took him into the hut where a native sergeant in
uniform checked his passport and offered him a lift to
Bisaka when he went back in his jeep to the barracks there.
Laver stayed behind at the airstrip on some business of his
own, but as Sinclair was about to leave, he said, "There's
only one hotel. The Bomu. You'll get a room there. My
wife, Lise, runs it." He grinned suddenly and went on, "I
daresay she'll make a bit of a pass at you. I don't blame
her. Makes a change from me. But I don't encourage it.
O.K.?"

"Don't worry."

He thought about Laver as he drove in alongside the
sergeant. Laver and his wife he recognised as part of his

world, always worn and frayed around the edges. Behind
him, miles away, was the lake and Nina ... there was
nothing sordid or shabby up there; just a wide stretch of
bright water and high mountains, clean and shining. He
wished he could have stayed there. Bisaka, he knew before he entered it, was going to give him a sour taste in the
mouth. The thought made him smile to himself. Maybe
the lake had put a spell on him.

\*     \*     \*

Most of the buildings in Bisaka were grouped around the
main, dusty, mud-packed square which was about the size
of a small football pitch. The military *caserne* was a mud
and plaster, single-storey, flat-roofed building with a
Central Africa flag flying over it. To one side of it were
the soldiers' quarters, two wooden barrack huts. Against
the wall of one now sat a row of off-duty men idly watching
the square where a handful of native boys played football
with a bright pink rubber ball. On the river side, where
the road ran through into the trees, were native huts and a
tall stretch of bamboo pallisade from behind which the
smoke of evening fires rose. The Hotel Bomu faced the
barracks from across the square. It was two storied,
wooden, and the green paint flaked from its boards like a
skin infection. A verandah ran along its front and there
was a small garden to one side of it.

The whole place looked worn-out and thoroughly dejected by the effort not of just getting through this fierce,
sun-smiting day, but of all the other thousands of days it
had known. A bullock cart came creaking up from the
river and the soldiers called insultingly to the man half
asleep on top of its load of sacks. The jeep dust still hung
hazily in the air as Sinclair went up the steps of the hotel,
and the evening shadows of the building lay long across the
square.

He came into the hotel, blinking a little against the
change of light from outside. It was a large room, bare

looking, with cane chairs and white-topped wooden tables. A black cast-iron stove with a pipe that went up to the ceiling and then across to an outer wall stood in the middle of the room. From a stairway on the far side of the room a bar ran in a short curve across one of the wall angles.

Two men sat at a table by one of the windows and there was a woman behind the bar. Over her head on the bar wall was a photograph of General de Gaulle, and another one of a coloured man in morning coat, holding a top hat in his hand, the President of the Central Africa Republic.

He dumped his pack and rifle at the foot of the bar. The woman, Laver's wife he guessed, was near her forties. She looked a bit worn and easy-going like everything else in the place.

"Good evening. A large whiskey, please. And I'd also like a room."

She nodded and as she turned to get the whiskey he saw that she had nice shoulders and her fresh silk blouse was tucked into a waist which was slimmer than he had expected.

She put the whiskey in front of him and said, "Sorry, no soda until next week, when the river boat comes up. Water?"

He nodded.

"How long will you be staying?"

"Some time I hope. Depends what I find here." He took the whiskey and sipped at it. The woman reached under the bar and then pushed the hotel register across to him. A small pencil, attached to a piece of string threaded into the book's spine, dangled loosely across the page. After a moment's hesitation he signed. *William Hadlow. Durban.*

The woman took the book, looked down at the name, nodded and smiled. And there it was, he had entered life again as William Hadlow.

She took him up to his room, going ahead of him. She flicked on the electric light, and seeing the surprise on his face, said, "Our own generators. Pete's supposed to look after them but they're always going wrong. How did you get here? There's no plane or boat in today from any-where?"

"Pete brought me in from the lake."

She straightened up from turning down the bed and stood close to him and just the way she stood told him that it would be easy to go on from there. Normally he might have done, but now he had Pete's words in his mind and beyond that sunlit memories of the lake and Nina. He pulled out his cigarettes and offered her one which she took, and he knew that she knew as he lit both cigarettes that it was the signing off moment. She smiled as she blew a cloud of smoke.

"Pete told you to be a good boy?"

"Yes. I'm here looking for a job. I'm a flyer like Pete."

"I see. You boys stick together, don't you? But that's all right. About the job—you ought to see Voyadis. He's down below now. I'll speak to him if you like."

"Thank you. What is he, Greek?"

"God knows. He's good natured so long as it doesn't cost him money. He could be worse. But then that goes for about everyone in this place. They could be worse. So Pete told you to be a good boy. Isn't that like you men. What would he say if I refused to let him have any whiskey?"

"Get it somewhere else, I dare say."

She laughed and went towards the door, but turned with it half open and said, "Dump your dirty clothes in the basket there—" She nodded towards the window. "I'll have them cleaned. If you need anything let me know. The mining company has a store by the river. I can get what you want."

When she was gone Sinclair stripped off his shirt and washed. Going down to the bar later, he found that only Lise was there.

"I spoke to Voyadis," she said. "He wants you to go up to his place after dinner for a drink."

\*　　\*　　\*

Solon Voyadis had a bungalow halfway along the road from Bisaka to the airstrip. It was a low shallow-roofed building, over-topped on one side by a large *tebeldi* tree. There was no garden, only a bare stretch of ground enclosed with a chain-link fence six feet high. Sinclair walked up there after his dinner. The night was warm and over the scrub along the road the fire-flies were pricking the night, their navigation lights flicking on and off.

The door of the bungalow opened as Sinclair reached it. He wasn't surprised because as he had pushed the entrance gate in the wire fence he had heard a bell ring somewhere in the house. Against the light stood a native girl, a *Fellata*, the red and yellow silk of her *firka* twisted tightly around her small waist and falling full over her ankles. She stood aside and motioned Sinclair to enter.

He went into a long, low room full of the smell of gabana coffee. The floor of the room was set with yellow and green tiles which shone under the oil lamps with a sleek glow. In the centre of the room was a long, low table of Arab iron-work, the top made from one massive run of marble. The chairs about it were native made, their seats thonged into a lattice work with strips of gazelle hide. Everything was well-kept and spotlessly clean. When Voyadis took a woman she was expected to work as well as to entertain him. Voyadis had brought the girl back from a trip over to El Muglad in the Sudan and she had cost him a lot of money.

Voyadis was sitting close to the table, a coffee tray, whiskey decanter, soda siphon and glasses near to his hand. He watched Sinclair come across the room, but did not rise. He waved a fat hand to a chair.

"Glad to meet you, Mr. Hadlow. Whiskey or coffee?"

"Coffee, thank you."

"Aroka."

The girl came forward and poured coffee for Sinclair, silver and gold bangles sliding on her arms as she lifted the cup and put it before him. When this was done Voyadis dismissed her.

"Pete Laver flew you in from the lake?"

"Yes."

"Was he drunk?"

Sinclair smiled. "Not a bit."

Voyadis smiled too and the whites of his eyes flashed broadly. He was a large man, a six-foot barrel of flesh, topped with a small round head with little, plump crinkles above the ears which ran into the semi-baldness of his grey-touched black hair. He wore a white silk suit with a black cummerbund and in one hand he held an ivory handled fly-whisk with a switch made from the long hairs of a zebra's mane. As he talked he kept tapping the handle of the whisk on the table or the fat of his leg.

"You're from Durban?"

"A long way back."

"And you turn up at the lake?"

"A man gets around the best he can."

Voyadis nodded. There was no point in asking awkward questions which wouldn't be answered truthfully. No man came up to Bisaka for the sake of his health. He liked the look of this man. He was used to looking at men and summing them up. This Hadlow sat, relaxed, but clearly master of himself. He looked straight at you with his hazel eyes, and on the sunburnt, squarish face there was the suggestion of a smile. But it was the kind of face that gave nothing away. .He wanted a job, but Voyadis was certain that he could never crawl for one. Whatever had brought him to Bisaka, it certainly wasn't drink. More likely a woman. He was the kind that women went for. Well, given time, he, Voyadis, might know. Meanwhile, company was hard to come by in Bisaka and it was good to have someone new to talk with.

"Lise tells me you want a job flying."

"I do, Mr. Voyadis. You run the air-transport company here, I understand."

"That. And some trading interests."

"What ships have you got?"

Voyadis told him; two Auster Aiglets and two D.H. 104 Doves.

"It is only a small affair. I have two pilots, Pete Laver and Henri Toubbu. Pete hits the bottle now and again and messes up routines. I could do with another man—so long as I don't have any drink problem with him."

"That's not my problem."

"Got a licence?"

"Yes."

"I see."

Voyadis was silent for a moment and helped himself to a glass of whiskey, then pushed the decanter across.

Then he said, "I'll pay you three hundred a week, and take care of your hotel board. A bonus every six months which runs between two hundred and fifty and three hundred and fifty new francs according to business."

"Fair enough. When do I start?"

"Tomorrow. But you'll have to clear your papers with Captain Suchard first."

"Who's he?"

"He's in charge of the military post here. Customs and so on as well."

"I thought that the French had cleared out of here? Just as the Belgians cleared out of the Congo."

"Not quite. The Republic here is only just getting going. There's an agreement that some French troops and police are left until things are really settled up. It's a helping hand to the Republic until they can manage things themselves. Meanwhile, nobody fusses too much."

"Meaning?"

"Well, the limits can be pushed a bit now and then. One of our main jobs is flying Mecca pilgrims over the hump to El Muglad."

Sinclair shrugged his shoulders. "I've only one rule, Mr. Voyadis. I don't take any load up unless I know I can bring it down—in one piece. O.K.?"

"You won't be asked to do more than that."

"What is this pilgrim business, anyway?"

Voyadis smiled and stirred heavily in his chair.

"It shows a nice profit—if you know how to handle it. Started me off in this business fifteen years ago. Then I was just a nobody Greek storekeeper down in Lassou. Now—in a few years I retire. Go back to Greece. Be a big, wealthy man . . ."

"Congratulations."

Voyadis smiled. "You're not interested in making a lot of money like that?"

"I've never had the chance. What is this pilgrim traffic —apart from the money in it."

"Ah, that. Yes, very interesting. Not many people know about it. Have another drink and I'll tell you."

Sinclair realised then that he had set Voyadis off on a hobby horse. He sat there listening, fascinated by what the man had to say, for this was an aspect of Africa which had so far escaped him.

Bisaka, Voyadis explained, itself had little importance. It stood on the northern bank of the Bomu river—a tributary of the Congo—and there were less than twenty Europeans in it. Two miles to the north of the town was a small gold mine and the gold was flown out once a month in one of Voyadis' planes to Bangui. Large stores and equipment usually came up the river by boat from Lassou. Down by the river there was a small cotton ginning mill, owned by the *Compagnie Cotonnerie Equatoriale Française*. Cotton and gold took most of the labour force. But Bisaka's real importance arose from the fact that it was on one of the main west to east pilgrim routes to Khartoum and so down to the Red Sea at Port Sudan and across to Mecca. The pilgrims came from as far west as Senegal, from the Gold Coast, from Nigeria, from the Cameroons

and from all the recently created Republics of Chad,
Gaboon, and the French Congo. From one year's end to
another a stream of pilgrims passed to and fro across the
great continent.

"They are like ants," said Voyadis. "Nothing stops
them for long. Once a man starts for Mecca then he
changes. From somewhere they get all the courage and
strength they need."

Sipping at his whiskey, Sinclair watched Voyadis'
large shining face as he talked on.

Many of the pilgrims, too poor to do otherwise, made
the entire journey on foot, sometimes taking as much as
five years. Others, less poor, used what transport they
could find. Only the really wealthy could afford to go all
the way by sea or air. Most of them worked their way
overland in small parties, the head of the party carrying
the pilgrim pass which gave details of all those travelling
with him, and when their money ran out they stopped and
worked until they had made enough for the next stage.
Bisaka was a favourite stopping place because of the gold
mine and cotton mill. From Bisaka eastwards lay the
hardest section of country for any pilgrim, across the
mountains that fanned away from the Massif de Tondou,
over the Djebel Mola and the Djebel Nougo into the tsetse-
plagued river land of the Bahr el Ghazal of the Sudan, and
from then on, six hundred and more miles, across the sand
and thorn wastes of the Sudan to El Obeid, the nearest rail-
head for Khartoum. Over this enormous stretch Voyadis
flew pilgrims. Not as far as El Obeid, but two hundred
miles short of it at a place called El Muglad from which
there was a reasonable road to El Obeid. Pilgrims were
careful with their money and once the vast mountain hump
was passed and they had a road before them they walked.

There was not a State in Africa which had any desire to
interfere with the pilgrim traffic. Frontier officials turned
a blind eye to lack of papers or passports. A man on his
way to Mecca needed no passport.

"And," said Voyadis, "every pilgrim has to have a clear bill of health before he goes from one country to another."

In Bisaka on the far side of the square was a pilgrim compound, maintained by Captain Suchard. Every pilgrim, going or coming, had to stay in it two weeks in order to be checked before moving on. At El Muglad there was a similar compound.

"They come here and they work and save until they have the money for the trip. Frankly, I pack 'em in like cattle. But they don't mind," said Voyadis. "Mecca is what they want. Except the women, of course—they're more interested in Jeddah, the port for Mecca."

At Jeddah, he explained, which meant "Grandmother", was the enormous grave where, according to Moslem tradition, Eve was buried, an object of special visitation by women, especially those desiring children. It was a long road to Mecca and children were born and old people died on the way, but to die on the way to Mecca was a blessed fate, bringing absolution for all sins. And all along the route for the thousands of miles between them and the Black Stone of the Ka'aba, where Adam after wandering for two hundred years over the face of the earth finally received God's pardon, unless they had their wits about them they were fleeced, robbed and cheated.

"But not by me," said Voyadis. "If they have the fare, I fly them. Some people I'll cheat willingly. But a pilgrim no. One does not make dishonest money out of religion. That would be unlucky. Pay the fare and fly. But not necessarily in luxury, eh?" He winked and laughed so that his huge body trembled all over. Then he went on, "It's a long, long flight to El Muglad and you need a strong nose and stomach to take it. You stay overnight there and then bring another load back. There are other, smaller jobs in between, and a fair amount of free time. O.K.?"

"It sounds fair enough to me."

"Good. By the way—was Major Winton up at the lake?"

"No. Only his daughter. He was away on safari."

"Oh, was he." Voyadis' face was thoughtful for a moment. Then he nodded at the decanter. "Have another before you go."

*       *       *

The next morning Sinclair took his passport and flying licence across to Captain Suchard. Suchard's office in the *caserne* was a bare little cell with one window that looked out on to the inner courtyard of the barracks. On the wall behind his desk was a picture of Marshal Lyautey under whom Suchard had served as a very young cavalry officer in Morocco in 1924. Suchard was a thin, worn-looking man of almost sixty whom age had ceased to mark for the last ten years. He was an Africa man, one of those who had given and sacrificed everything to the country, and one of those who could never leave it because dedication had passed into habit and the habit could never be broken.

He examined the passport and the flying licence, made no comment and pushed them back to Sinclair. Then he looked up at him and said, "What made you come to Bisaka, monsieur?"

For a moment Sinclair hesitated. Then, since this man had at once commanded his respect, he said frankly, "I had trouble where I was working. A change seemed a good thing."

"What kind of trouble?"

"A woman."

Suchard smiled thinly. "Women, drink, or a police record. Those are the qualifications for Bisaka. I've been here enough years to know that. Why did you pick Bisaka?"

"I'd heard about it. Knew there was an air-transport company. I don't care for the big outfits. Voyadis seems to have struck a good thing in this pilgrim business."

"He has other businesses, too. Don't get mixed up in them."

"Maybe you should make that clearer?"

"Why not—it is no secret. He flies pilgrims over and back. Pilgrims are human beings. And not all of them are going to Mecca. Anyone can say he is a pilgrim, and then for himself or for Voyadis he takes over stuff . . . drugs, narcotics, gold, diamonds . . . anything which will fetch a higher price somewhere else. Sometimes we find the stuff, monsieur. Mostly we don't. But never is Voyadis directly concerned. I tell you this for your own good — don't get mixed up in it."

"Thanks for the advice. I just want to fly."

"Good."

Sinclair went back to the hotel. From there Pete Laver took him up to the airstrip in one of the company's jeeps. On the way up, he said, "Suchard give you a warning? Smuggling and all that?"

"Yes."

"Well—it's up to you. It goes on, of course. If you want to make more on the side, then just say so to Voyadis."

"Is it worth it?"

"I think so. Anything to get Lise and myself out of this hole some time. Not interested?"

Sinclair shook his head. "Well, I'll take it easy for a bit. Thanks all the same."

"O.K. Bill. No one's going to press you."

# CHAPTER FIVE

W HEN they had found the plane, Mabenge's men had dived and got ropes fixed to the undercarriage. It had been dragged from the river and up the rough slope of the bank, which had been cleared of trees and shrubs for thirty yards back into the forest. The light plane sat now on the bank with one broken wing trailing away to the ground, the mud hard baked over it.

Out in the river some of Mabenge's men were standing to their breasts in the turbid water, shouting and beating at the surface with sticks, while inside their ring other men dived and searched the river bed. That Mabenge had taken his place in the ring of men did not surprise Winton. He never asked his men to do what he would not do himself. There was always the chance that some crocodile would be unimpressed by the noise, some rogue beast with a deep hatred of men who would come sliding in and pick one of them off.

Winton had a deep affection and respect for the Azandes. Although they were less touched by civilisation than many other tribes, they had a great tradition of conquest and military prowess. They were a fine people and, if time had dimmed a little the qualities of courage, loyalty and fitness which had once made them great, these were still there, waiting to be drawn out and hardened into a bright virtue again.

For Winton courage, loyalty and fitness were the great virtues. It was from these that men shaped their destinies, from these that men made themselves powerful. No other virtues mattered.

He got up from where he was sitting and walked im-

58

patiently over to the plane. It had taken them over two weeks to find it.

The long reach of the Ebola here was crowded right up to the bank with trees, and it was about a hundred yards wide. Some way below the men in the river was a narrow sand bar. It was not difficult for Winton to see what Hadlow had been planning, after the trouble started. Hadlow would keep his head, and he knew the danger of crocodiles. A landing among the trees would have smashed him to pieces. He had tried to land just off the sand bar so that he could get on to it with only two or three yards to go. He could not land on the bar itself. It was too small. He must have been losing height rapidly as he made his first run over. Winton's eyes went to a large tree that overhung the bank just below the Azandes. Part of it had been smashed and ripped away where Hadlow, too much height lost, had hit it on the first run in. The plane had dropped into the water a hundred yards higher up than the sandbar, settling into eight or ten feet of water.

What had happened to Hadlow then, he wondered? He might have been unconscious, but at least in the cockpit he would have his head above water. When he came to he would have had twenty yards to go to make the bank. He would have made that all right. But why the devil hadn't he stopped with the plane? The fool. They'd put men out along the bank but no trace of him had been found. If only people would obey orders.

The shouting and beating in the river stopped and Mabenge with his men, the water dripping from their black nakedness, came up the bank. Mabenge stopped by Winton and, picking up his shirt and trousers, began to pull them on over his wet body.

"There is nothing there, major."

"I didn't expect anything. If he had been killed he would have still been in the cockpit. He got out and took the stuff with him."

"We've found no tracks."

"It was a storm that brought him down. Rain. They'd be washed out long before we got here. From here up to the lake these are all your people. You must send out the word to them to look for him. He must be found, dead or alive."

Mabenge said firmly, "He will be found."

A flock of paroquets crossed the river, looping their way above the sand bar. From the middle of the stream the knuckled forehead of a crocodile rose and drifted with the current for a moment.

Winton said, "Send out your messages, and we'll head back. For all we know Hadlow may be waiting at the lake for us."

He moved away from Mabenge down to the river. The chocolate coloured flood swept past him and he watched it, seeing it as time passing, waiting for no man. But as rapidly as it passed there was more to come, an endless flood of time. It was only man who had a term set to his days . . . only so much time in which to do the things he must do. Momentarily the ambition in him was like an anger . . . a man had to make his mark, dream and then shape his dream as hard fact. Between them, he and Mabenge were going to make their mark no matter how small the beginning . . . the shape of greatness and power lay ahead, the promise of it waiting for them.

*    *    *

At the airstrip Pete Laver introduced Sinclair to the other pilot Henri Toubbu and to the ground crew, and the mechanics. Henri, an Egyptian who had come from Cairo to Voyadis when the service first started, was a tall, thin, nervous mannered man with a soft voice. He took Sinclair over to one of the D.H. 104 Doves that stood outside the far hangar.

"You know these?"

"Yes. Flown them in Tanganyika." He had to keep clear in his mind that he was Hadlow not Sinclair, and that his past history must be shaped accordingly. Actually he had flown them in Uganda. They were good, sturdy, workaday planes. This one looked as though it had had its share of work days, too. But you couldn't tell just by looking. In a minute he would know when the two 305 h.p. D.H. Gypsy Queen engines opened up.

He climbed in with Henri. The fuselage was just a shell right back to the tail compartment. Henri saw his look and smiled.

"No comforts."

A few moments later he was trundling her out on to the airstrip. He taxi-ed up to the end, turned, and began to run the engines up. She answered nicely and, as he felt the shake of her against the bite of the brakes, some part of him which had been sleeping for days came awake. It was good to be sitting up in the nose, a wide runway ahead and the sky waiting. What the hell was there in a name, so long as you could get off the ground again? And some one around here was good with engines. She was growling and ready to go, full of appetite like himself.

He took her up and, without pushing her, put her through her steps and he liked her. He made three landings to get the feel of the strip and the second time as he gunned her off again he saw Voyadis standing outside the office building door watching him. As they came in gently for the last time, Henri at his side sighed and shook his head.

"I can live for as long as I like, but never will I be your way. Somewhere it is not with me, not in the hands or the head."

Back in the office Voyadis said to him, "O.K. I've seen enough. Tomorrow you can do the El Muglad run. I'll send Amra with you. He's only a boy but he knows the ropes. If you let him take over it's your responsibility. Not that he isn't capable, but he's got no certificate."

As he spoke Voyadis reached into his desk drawer and then slid a Baby Browning ·25 across to him. "Sign for this."

"What the hell do I want that for?"

Pete Laver by the window laughed at his surprise.

"For the pilgrims, Bill. Sometimes when you get 'em up there one of 'em is likely to panic. Never been in a plane before. It can be infectious. Just show the gun and they calm down. I had to shoot one bastard in the leg a month ago."

"Strictly on loan. Company property," said Voyadis as Sinclair signed.

"The women are the worse," went on Pete. "They get sick all over the place."

That evening Sinclair played bridge with Suchard, Pete and Voyadis. He and Pete lost money to the other pair, largely because as the evening went on Pete became tighter and tighter and finally, at the end of a rubber, abandoned the game and went out into the square for some fresh air. Captain Suchard and Voyadis left. There were a few other people in the room when Sinclair, knowing he had an early start in the morning, went up to his room. He was standing by the window when there was a knock on the door.

Lise came in.

"You're off to El Muglad tomorrow?"

"Yes."

"Then you'd better take a couple of blankets with you and a tin of flea powder."

"Thanks, Lise. I will." Then jerking his cigarette end through the window, not looking at her, he said, "He's got to fly down to Lassou tomorrow with stores. Will he be fit?"

Her voice unconcerned, too unconcerned, she said, "He'll be fit."

"What's it all about? He's a nice guy. He shouldn't do it to himself. And one of these days he'll think he's fit and he won't be. I've seen it happen."

"I know. But we have to be the way we are. There's no arguing about that."

There was nothing pathetic about her. She stood there, an attractive woman still who had the virtue of accepting things that couldn't be altered.

"I suppose not."

"It's just a question of what the things are. They show in Pete. They show in me. But not in you. But I don't care who it is—there's always something. Now shut that window or the place will be full of mosquitoes."

He lay in bed thinking about her remarks before he slept. Everybody had some defect. Was it true? It certainly was. Himself, he knew that he was too damned easy-going. If things or places didn't please him, then he found a way out. It made life a damned sight simpler but where did it get you in the end?

When he slept his dreams were untroubled, sunlit and bright with the shimmer of blue water around a green island and there was a girl in them, pale blonde hair loose, who danced on a golden beach in a white swim suit with a slate grey and green python wrapped around her arms and shoulders like a scarf which, for his money, seemed a hell of a way to waste a sunny day on an island beach.

\*     \*     \*

One of Voyadis' clerks with a coloured sergeant of Captain Suchard's post supervised the pilgrims as they went aboard. The plane originally was designed to carry eleven or twelve passengers. Twenty pilgrims with their bundles of personal possessions were jammed into the plane.

A length of wide-mesh rope netting about three feet high was drawn across the back of the control department and the pilgrims were not allowed forward of this. They settled in the length of the fuselage, squatting on their bundles and all suddenly quiet once they were in the plane. For most of them this was their first trip in a plane and they were full of suspicion and fear. They were a mixed bunch of men and women and a few children . . . Singalese,

Nigerians, Arabs from the Lake Chad district, and Congo-
lese coming up from the south-west. They looked like
a bunch of refugees, for throughout the pilgrimage they
wore only their poorest clothes, except for the final stage
to Mecca when they wore the two sheets which were all
that a pilgrim was allowed. And coming back they would
look like refugees until they were on the outskirts of their
homes and there they would bring out from their bundles
new clothes and gaily coloured scarves and then, with the
men wearing the round, coloured hats of woven straw
which mark the *hajji*, make a joyful entry to be greeted by
their friends and relatives.

Sinclair ran the machine up to the end of the runway
and as he gunned up the motors he looked back and saw a
woman being sick on the floor. A strong stomach and a
strong nose, somebody had said. He smiled to himself.
A couple of children began to wail and some of the elders,
taking comfort in the sound, began to intone aloud, half-
wailing, half-singing. As he waited for the signal from the
little tower above the office buildings, Sinclair realised
that there were a lot of things which he would never
understand. What was it that burned steadily inside these
people and made them take this long, long journey?

Behind him he could hear Amra's voice now, shouting
and bullying at the pilgrims, giving them orders and pro-
hibitions in a strange mixed up language and he smiled
to himself as he heard Amra repeating that no fires were
to be lit. Apparently some of the pilgrims in the past
had had the idea that it was in order for them to light
a fire on the floor and prepare a meal during the long
journey.

Sinclair took the Dove down the runway and lifted her
gently. They flew at two thousand feet, following for a
while the line of the Bomu river eastwards. Sinclair had
spent an hour in the office before the flight, studying the
maps and getting into his mind a picture of the journey.
He had a good memory and once the map was in his mind

it stayed there and when he was aloft the ground below became the map, eyes and mind fusing the two.

Amra came forward from the pilgrims and squatted beside him. He was about eighteen, a thin slip of long-legged awkwardness who, now that the pilgrims had been suitably impressed, kept giving little grunts of pleasure at being in the air. He wore bush shorts and a sleeveless green pullover ballooning over a red and white striped football jersey and on his head was a red beret with his name worked in white beads on the crown. Sinclair could see it as the boy squatted below him. He grinned to himself. It was obviously for identification only from the air. He liked Amra and his grunts, knowing only too well his pleasure. It was good to be up here with the whole sky ahead and above.

Way ahead of them the river began to break slowly from its eastward course and turn northwards. Sinclair should have followed it but instead he kept going eastwards until through the blue haze he saw the peaks of a mountain range begin to eat up into the sky.

At his side Amra said, "You not follow the river, mister?"

"Not for the moment, Amra. Don't worry."

"Sometimes, Mister Laver let me take over, only for a small while," said Amra casually, staring straight ahead.

Sinclair chuckled. "You a good flyer, Amra?"

"Pretty good, sir."

"We'll see a bit later, when we get over the hump. Meantime grab this and be ready to let it go when I say."

He reached into his pocket and pulled out a round cigarette tin, the lid secured with a strip of tape. As Amra took it, puzzled, Sinclair gave a touch on the rudder, swinging south, seeing the mountains coming up on his port side. He looked down at the steep slopes, at the bare rock and tumbled morraines that died away into the thick, green carpet of trees.

He cleared the crests of the hills and then did a slow

turn from the south and there below him was the lake. He came down low over N'Dene's homestead and then was running at five hundred feet above the strip of lake shore towards Winton's camp. The waters of the lake because of some trick of light were black, black as ebony with the vivid green of the islands against it. A handful of flamingoes rose and streamed out to their right, a small pink and white cloud.

"Flamingo," said Amra. "Mister Laver hit one once."

"Not me, Amra. O.K. Get ready to drop it."

Ahead of them now was the collection of tents and huts and he saw the figures of two or three native boys and then, clear in the sunshine, the pale gleam of blonde hair as Nina came from one of the huts that held the caged animals, looking upwards.

"Now."

He gave a waggle of his wings and was climbing, hard and fast for the mountains that framed the northern end of the lake bow. He heard Amra chuckle, felt the blast of air shut off as the side window scuttle was closed.

"Was it a good shot, Amra?"

"Right on the beach, sir."

"Good boy."

"Yes, sir." Amra grunted and then grinning all over his face said, "One day I fly a plane like that, sir. I come in like that for my girl friend to see, and all the birds look up and say, 'That boy's one flyer'."

"You will, Amra. You're learning fast."

Amra's face clouded.

"Mister Voyadis—he be damned mad, sir, if he knew you did this loop off course."

"Is he going to know, Amra?"

Amra grinned. "Not from me, sir. Not from me."

As they flew on he was trying to picture Nina on the beach, imagining her face as she picked up the tin with his letter. While he had been composing it, he had been thinking about Nina and the lake, and he had had the odd feeling—looking round the shabby dining room of the Bomu Hotel—that he could easily have dreamt the whole thing. There was no lake, no Nina. It was a new experience for him to have a place and a person take such importance in his mind. Usually places were places, people were people, and they were always changing and being soon forgotten. This new feeling had made him want his letter to be important but he had found that hard to bring off. In fact, he had had to settle for something far short of his intentions. The pencil in his hand had seemed to paralyse his emotions. The letter read:

Good morning, beautiful. Have got a job in Bisaka. See you on my first day off. Love, Bill.

It was no damned good at all. Too short, and not saying anything that he really felt. What he would have liked to have done would have been to write her a real love letter, something a girl would stick to until it went dog-eared and finally fell apart.

*     *     *

El Muglad was a loneliness, lost in an endless plain of yellow sand where nothing much but thorn and dom palms grew. There were a few grass-thatched native huts, a couple of guest bungalows, the airstrip and a pilgrim compound, the whole place under command of a Sudanese *Mamur*. The settlement was fly- and flea-ridden and Sinclair couldn't wait to get out of it.

Once they had cleared the mountains, Sinclair had given Amra a spell at the controls and the boy had handled the ship very well. Amra had been delighted.

Amra looked after him in the bungalow, made his bed and got to work with the flea powder, and then went off to clean up the ship. And it needed cleaning up, for the passage over the Massif de Tondou had been bumpy and gone straight to the pilgrims' stomachs.

At the airstrip there was a small bar and canteen and

when Sinclair went over there for a drink and a meal he met the Sudanese *Mamur* who introduced him to an Egyptian who had come down on the Khartoum plane that morning and wanted a passage to Bisaka.

The man was called Hussein Nahud. He was a small brown nut of a man, his Arab ancestry clear in the lean, thin face with its sharp nose and dark, large eyes. He was wearing an over-sized blue pin-striped city suit that looked as though it had seen other owners and from the breast pocket protruded the caps of an assortment of pencils and pens. On one wrist he wore an enormous gold watch which he kept jerking back his cuff to consult as though his life were full of numerous appointments all of which, from the worried expression on his face, he fancied he was going to miss.

When they were introduced, he said, "Mr. Hadlow . . . Ah, yes. Ah, yes," and then took a look at his watch as though to indicate that he could only spare him a few seconds. In fact he stayed and had three drinks with them before going off to his night's quarters in the other guest bungalow.

Amra woke Sinclair early the next morning with coffee brought over from the canteen. He stood by and lit Sinclair's cigarette and then fussed around heating up some shaving water on a small spirit stove. When Sinclair began to shave in the small cubicle which adjoined the bedroom Amra stood in the doorway watching him.

Amra said, "You going to stay in Bisaka a long time, boss?"

"Quite a while, Amra."

"I try to work with you always, boss. Then I get plenty of flying, yes?"

"Could be, Amra."

"You know this passenger we take back today, boss?"

"Who? Nahud?"

"Yes, boss."

"No."

"He's very interested in you, boss. Ask me about you."

"Oh? What sort of things?"

"How long you been with us. Where you come from."

Sinclair looked round, razor poised.

"What did you tell him?"

"I tell him the truth, boss. This your first flight and you come from lake, from Miss Winton. Everyone know that."

"Perhaps he's just one of these curious types, Amra. Got to know everything about other people's business."

He was not worried about Hussein Nahud. But he was a little curious himself at the news that the man had been making enquiries about him. In the bar, where they had taken a few drinks together, Nahud had said that he was a cotton buyer going to Bisaka on business.

"You ever seen this man in Bisaka before, Amra?"

"No, boss."

Later, on his way over to the plane, he saw Nahud standing a little aside from the pilgrims who were entering the plane. Why, he wondered, had the man asked Amra the questions about him? They were simple, straightforward questions that he could have asked him direct. Perhaps Nahud didn't like to be direct. He didn't look the kind who would go frankly and directly about any kind of business. However, his curiosity, whatever its motive, was kept in hand during the flight back to Bisaka. He sat on a small packing case up against the netting and slept most of the time. The flight went without trouble and Sinclair was at Bisaka by the late afternoon.

One of Suchard's men came across to marshal the pilgrims and Sinclair sat relaxed in his seat watching them get out. An old man, shuffling stiffly to the door, looked at him, bowed and touched his forehead in salute. Through the open door the heat from the strip beat into the plane and intensified the smell of vomit. There was nothing B.O.A.C. about this run, thought Sinclair. This lot would turn a stewardess's hair white in a couple of trips. Hussein Nahud, clutching a slim briefcase, went out after the last pilgrim, pausing at the door to say, "Thank you, Captain Hadlow, for a pleasant flight."

"You're welcome."

When the plane was clear, Sinclair went across to Voyadis' office. Voyadis was there, sitting at his desk, and greeted him with a wave of his fly-whisk.

"Good trip?"

"So-so. Wouldn't it be a good idea to dish 'em out with paper sacks or some buckets to be sick in?"

"I've tried that. They just steal the buckets and they think the paper sacks are too useful to waste that way. Easier to give the plane a good wash-out."

# CHAPTER SIX

THAT evening Sinclair played bridge with Captain Suchard, Voyadis and Laver. But about nine o'clock Suchard was called away to deal with some trouble which had arisen in the pilgrim compound. The game was broken up and Sinclair decided to get an early night. Tomorrow was his day off and he had already made plans for an early start.

He went upstairs to his room. When he entered, it was to find Hussein Nahud leaning over his bed, on which lay his pack, rifle and the bandolier of ammunition.

Nahud, one hand still on the pack, jerked round nervously and then, almost reproachfully, looked at his watch as though it had let him down over the timing of Sinclair's movements. He opened his mouth slowly as though making a painful choice of words to be used, but before he could say anything Sinclair moved across the room and grabbed him by the loose stuff of his jacket. He gave him a quick shake and said, "You bloody little bazaar thief!"

He forced the man towards the window and with his free hand opened it. Then before Nahud could say anything Sinclair picked him up and tossed him out into the night. It was a twelve foot drop. There was a crash of breaking shrubs and a cry. Sinclair closed the window and went to the bed. Nahud had almost finished putting things back into the pack when he had been disturbed. Sinclair did not bother to check over his possessions. There was nothing there he would miss. His money and passport he carried in his jacket which he was wearing.

He picked up the pack from the bed and walked with it to his wardrobe. As he turned away there was a knock on his door.

"Come in."

The door opened slowly and Nahud came partly around it. He looked nervous, but there was a curious flicker of determination in the large, black eyes.

Sinclair frowned.

"You've got a damned nerve, coming back here!"

Nahud slid round the door and then closed it. He gave a nervous little cough and smiled anxiously.

"Please, Mr. Hadlow . . ." One hand went up defensively as Sinclair moved towards him. "Don't be impetuous again. I'm sorry I was so foolish just now. . . ." He broke off and rubbed his right arm and Sinclair saw that the sleeve had been ripped in his fall. "You could have broken one of my arms or legs, dropping me like that, Mr. Hadlow."

"It ought to have been your neck."

Nahud frowned, as though this was a thought which had not occurred to him. One hand went up and adjusted his row of pen and pencil caps. He said, "Actually it was my watch I was most worried about. It is a very expensive watch."

"No doubt. And probably stolen. What were you after in my room?"

"I wanted to look at your passport, Mr. Hadlow."

"What the hell for?"

"Because I like to check everything. You see, I know that your real name can't be Hadlow."

"It damned well is. Who the devil are you?"

The anger in Sinclair's voice made Nahud's eyes blink apprehensively, but he shook his head and raised one paw-like hand in a placatory gesture.

"Please, Mr. Hadlow, let me say something. I am not personally concerned with your private affairs . . . you can be what you choose to people like Mr. Voyadis or Captain Suchard . . ." He paused, frowned a little as though he knew that he hadn't framed his approach delicately enough, and then tried again. "What I mean is that anything we say to one another in this room will be entirely confidential. You have your life to live and I have mine."

"So it would seem."

Nahud smiled, as though something had been absolutely agreed between them, and said, "I know that you are not Mr. Hadlow. I have seen many photographs of him. I hear a lot about him. But all I want to know is—where is the real Mr. Hadlow?"

For a moment Sinclair said nothing. But he was thinking—Would you believe it? He hadn't been in this dump more than a few days and already somebody had rumbled him.

Sinclair said, "You're talking nonsense. I'm Hadlow. Now get out."

But Nahud was in and this time meant to stay in, Sinclair could read that under the man's nervous manner.

"Please be patient with me," said Nahud. "I do not ask for your reasons for taking Hadlow's name. I just want to know where he is. Also, I do not ask you to tell me this freely. This knowledge is important to me and I am ready to pay for it. But not much, Mr. Hadlow. I am not a rich man. Just tell me where he is or how I can find him and I will pay you a hundred pounds."

"You're a persistent little bastard, aren't you? What's all this about anyway?"

Nahud shrugged his shoulders. "You keep your reasons private. I do the same. The simple fact is that I will pay you for information about Hadlow."

"And suppose I tell you that you're absolutely wrong. That I'm Hadlow, always have been? What happens then?" He was curious now and cautious. This little man might be able to make trouble. Also, a hundred pounds was a lot of money.

Nahud looked down at his watch, polished the glass with the edge of his sleeve and then, looking back at Sinclair, gave him a friendly smile.

"Nothing—officially, Mr. Hadlow. We all of us have to live. Why should I make your life more difficult by exposing you to Captain Suchard? Indeed, I am offering you a chance to make your life pleasanter."

"It sounds too easy."

"You simply tell me where he is." Nahud put his hand inside his jacket and pulled out a fat wallet. "I have not the money in pound notes. But I have the equivalent in American dollars. Let's see, say three dollars to the pound. Three hundred dollars. Actually you make a little more than a hundred pounds because the dollar is strictly—"

"Look—don't bother with the exchange rates. Who is this other Hadlow and why do you want him?"

Nahud considered this for a while. Quite clearly, being a reasonable man, his whole manner declared, he took the point. In Sinclair's place he would be just as cautious and non-committal.

"All I can tell you is this. So far as you are concerned, taking Hadlow's name will mean nothing to anyone in Bisaka. But anywhere else . . . it might get you into trouble."

"Well now, is that so?"

"It is so." Nahud smiled. "You are not interested in a hundred pounds?"

"Of course I am."

"Between ourselves—you are not Hadlow."

Sinclair hesitated for a moment. There was no point in pretending. The worst that could happen anyway if Nahud talked was that he would have to move on.

"No, I'm not."

Nahud nodded. It was clear that his nervousness was gone; that he felt now at ease and, indeed, perhaps master of the situation. He shuffled the dollar bills absently through his fingers.

"He is dead?"

"Yes, he's dead."

"Not killed?"

Sinclair smiled. Nahud was on the ball. And he had the feeling that if he had killed Hadlow, Nahud would not have been surprised.

"No. Dead—by natural means. And buried by me."

"I see. . . . And somewhere not a long way away? You see, before I can pay the money, I must be absolutely certain of his death. I must see the grave and identify him."

"I don't see why. You can take my word for it."

"Nevertheless, I must see the grave. Not that I would doubt your word. But, as you may have guessed, I am only a servant of others in this and they are not the kind of people who would continue to employ me if I took such a thing as this on trust. I must see him, Mr. Hadlow. And then the money is yours. You remember where you buried him, of course."

"There's no *of course* about it. It was just country to me. It all looks alike around here."

Nahud split the fan of bills neatly in half and, smiling, put one of them on the bed by Sinclair. "One hundred and fifty now. And the rest when you take me to the grave."

Sinclair took the bills and handed them back.

"Now, don't rush me."

Some of Nahud's earlier nervousness returned.

"Now, Mr. Hadlow, don't say that you're not going to help me—"

"I'm not saying that." Sinclair gave him a warm smile. "It just is that I'm not a man who rushes into things, Nahud. Let's face it"—he saw Nahud's mouth droop with concern—"any reasonable man would want to sleep on a thing like this. Don't you agree?"

"Well . . ."

"Of course you do." Sinclair moved towards the door. "We'll talk about it again tomorrow, Nahud. Good night."

Nahud hesitated for a moment, opened his mouth as

though to say something, and then went out without a
word.

\*　　\*　　\*

Alone in his room Sinclair went to the window, lit a
cigarette and stared out into the night. He didn't care a
damn that Nahud knew he wasn't Hadlow. Even if he
let Suchard know, the worst that could come of it was a
fine, or a week in clink, and then he would have to move
on. Too bad.

The real point was, what was all this Hadlow business?
And why did Nahud have to see the body? Why not take
his word for Hadlow's death? And who the hell was
Nahud, anyway? He'd have been a fool just to grab the
hundred pounds without another thought. Nahud, he
fancied, had been a bit too quick in offering it. Damn it,
for the sake of keeping his secret he might have been
expected to take him to Hadlow's grave for nothing. But
the money had been offered. And, let's face it, he told
himself, a man never offered the top price right away. He
could take Nahud to a hundred and fifty pounds for sure.

Anyway, it would be easy money. The grave was in the
mountains somewhere beyond the far end of the lake. It
shouldn't be difficult to find. In a way the visit of Nahud
was well timed. Tomorrow he could kill two birds with
one stone . . . if that was the right way to think about a
visit to Nina at the lake.

He turned away from the window. Well, there was
nothing he could do about it tonight. The rifle and the
cartridge bandolier lay on his bed still. He reached over
and picked them up and was turning away with them
when something on the broad white band of turned-down
sheet at the top of the bed where the bandolier had rested
caught his eyes.

He bent over and examined it and saw that it was a thin
speckling of black dust which trailed across the top of the
sheet following the line on which he had dragged the

bandolier from the bed. He raised the bandolier in his left hand and holding it over the sheet gave it a shake. The faintest spill of black powder trickled downwards to the sheet.

Sinclair sat down on the bed with the bandolier across his knees. Well, now, what the hell was this? Slowly he opened the pouch from which the powder had come. It held four twelve-bore shotgun cartridges. He pulled them out and as he rolled them on his hand he saw that the cardboard wad at the end of one was not quite in place. Black gunpowder leaked on to his palm. Or was it gunpowder? He took the cartridges over to his table and spilled a little more of the powder into his tin ash-tray. Then he dropped a lighted matchstick on to it—and jumped back, swearing, about three feet. It was gunpowder all right!

Sitting on his bed again he went through the rest of the ammunition in the bandolier. Most of it was ·303 stuff for the rifle, but there were a dozen twelve-bore cartridges. Hadlow had probably had another gun. Lost it maybe in the plane smash. Each of the twelve-bore cartridges, Sinclair saw, had had the cardboard wad at the tip taken off and then put back. He could see the bruising made by a knife point on each. And it hadn't been a very neat job. The man who had done it—and he wasn't giving himself three guesses to name him—had been damned inefficient.

Methodically Sinclair prized loose the wads with his own knife and tipped the contents into the ash-tray. There was nothing in them except gunpowder and shot. None of the ·303 bullets had been touched.

Thoughtfully, he gathered up the ash-tray and went out of his room and along to the lavatory where he flushed the powder away. He didn't want some maid of Lise's to take the stuff from his bedroom in the morning and chuck it on the hotel stove.

Back in his room, he put his feet up on the bed and went through his pack which he had fetched from the wardrobe. Everything there was in order.

He whistled to himself gently. His instinct had been right when he had said he wanted to sleep on all this, refusing to be rushed. A hundred pounds, eh? Just for checking that the dead man was really Hadlow. Nahud must have thought that he was well stuck with the bridge game for hours. He could see him, working away, glancing nervously at his watch no matter how much time he felt he had. So now, what did it add up to? Plenty of odd things went on in this country. As a pilot he had more than once been asked to do things which were never explained . . . just tuck a parcel into your jacket and hand it over to a man at such-and-such airport. Simple. Money paid and no explanations. Usually—unless he had been hard up—he had kept clear of such affairs. Had Hadlow been carrying something for Nahud? Something small that might conceivably have been hidden in a large cartridge. Or more than one cartridge. Drugs, diamonds, microfilms . . . whatever it was, it was worth money. And he was being offered a hundred pounds to lead Nahud to it. Interesting. Whatever it was he was sure that he was on the wrong end of a bad bargain. He would be a fool not to reverse the positions.

He jerked his cigarette through the open window and slewed his feet off the bed. Leaning over to undo his shoes he was telling himself that he wouldn't fix any price until he knew more. The first thing he had to do was to make sure where the grave was.

\*     \*     \*

He was up early the next morning. Suchard's sergeant went out to the airstrip at seven in the morning and Sinclair had arranged to have a lift up with him.

Lise served his breakfast and towards the end came and sat down with him over a cup of coffee.

Sinclair said, "Ever seen this Nahud who's staying here before?"

Lise shook her head. Then she gave him an upward,

curious glance. "The servants tell me you caught him in your room last night and dropped him out of the window."

"How could they know that?"

Lise shrugged her shoulders. "My boys know everything." Then with fresh interest in her voice, she went on, "It's your day off, isn't it?"

"Yes."

"So why the early start?"

Sinclair smiled. "I'm taking a trip out to the lake."

"Since when were you interested in flamingoes?"

"Been a bird-watcher for years."

A car horn blew outside and a few moments later Sinclair was on his way to the airstrip, a long cloud of dust trailing away behind the car.

Henri Toubbu was in the office.

Sinclair gave him a good-morning and then pulled out the map of the lake area from the map shelf. He sat down and began to study it carefully. He knew that he could not have travelled a great distance with the malaria on him after he had left Hadlow. He felt that he could place the location of the grave within an area of about five square miles. And there was the landmark of the great pile of flat rocks, like stacked plates, to help him. It was not shown on the map.

Henri, interested in his study of the map, said, "What are you doing up here today?"

"Going for a trip."

"What in?"

"The spare Auster Aiglet. They aren't both being used, are they?"

"No. But that doesn't mean you can use one."

"Why not?"

"Voyadis doesn't let us pilots use the planes except for official trips."

"I'll pay for the petrol if that's what's worrying him."

"He doesn't care about the petrol. No private flips. That's his order."

"Orders were made to be broken."

"You'll be in trouble."

"I'm used to it. And if it makes it any easier—you had no idea what I was going to do. Just walked in and took off before you could do anything. O.K.?"

Sinclair went over to the first hangar and found Amra. It took him ten minutes to make it clear to Amra that he was flying alone and, when he did take-off, he could see the red beret below him, a black face upturned and no doubt watching with envy.

He banked the Auster slowly over Bisaka, saw the thin curls of cooking fire smoke from the pilgrim compound, a squad of soldiers drilling in the yard behind the *caserne*, and then he was away following the looping line of the tree-crowded Bomu. The Auster had a range of nearly five hundred and fifty miles. More than he would need by far. And the two tanks were full. It was just over an hour's flight to the lake. He had all the time in the world.

Down below he saw a fish-hawk circling over the river and remembered Nina telling him about the fish-hawk at the lake. Looking down now there was no sign of any human life at all . . . just a vast stretch of forest to the south and then, north of the river, the trees breaking away and the yellow, sandy plain running into a haze of mist and sky. It was a big country, all right. Just plain bloody big. And the whole thing was beginning to stir and would take some handling. So far he hadn't been impressed by any of the handling he had seen. Both black and white politicians seemed happy to walk about the ammunition dump smoking. Politics. . . . There was a possibility, he supposed, that Nahud and the dead Hadlow had some political tie-up. There was money to be made in politics in Africa these days.

The Auster bumped a bit in an air-pocket and he nursed her, pulling her up. The mountains ahead were beginning to show now, looking first like steely grey clouds low on the skyline, then fast taking a hardness, sharp and

shadowed by the sun. He eased around to the south and
flew in low, keeping below the crests, running down their
flanks about a mile from them.

He made a ten mile run down the line of the mountains,
keeping at a respectable distance. Then he came back,
edging closer into them, and just after he had turned he
found what he was looking for, the one landmark, the
spur running boldly out from the slope with great layers
of rock piled on its nose. He went over it at about a
thousand feet and had time to see the deep gully in dark
shadow from the sun. He could not pick out the mouth of
the cave. But he knew it was there. This place could not
be mistaken.

He could not land near it either. There was nowhere to
make a landing on this side of the mountains. He made
another turn south and then put the nose up and crossed
the peaks. On the other side the line of crests were revealed as a long run of broken plateau, curving in a great
crescent back towards the lake which he could not see.
About four miles south of the spur which hid the cave the
mountain plateau widened. There were fewer rocks and
one or two patches of yellowed grass and shrub. He came
down low and saw a line of trees running off the plateau
northwards. Not far from the beginning of the trees the
ground looked reasonably flat. He went over it as low as
he dared and saw that there was just about enough room
to make a landing. But it wasn't the kind of landing he
was going to try out today. It only needed a hidden rock
or two in the grass and scrub and he could put the Auster
on its nose. Then there would be hell to pay with Voyadis.
Before he took that risk he wanted to be sure that it was
going to be worth it. He was looking forward to another
talk with Nahud.

He turned again and climbed, heading for the south end
of the lake and in a few moments its waters came into view.

Sinclair began to whistle to himself happily. He had a
day off, and a girl to visit. He'd more or less pinched the

boss's plane. And there was, obviously, some easy money
in the offing. That gave the whole thing added zest.

The mountainside began to fall away rapidly into the
lake bowl. He went down its southern slope and saw
N'Dene's homestead coming up fast below him. He
dropped lower and went over it, watching the plane
shadow race across the ground and small figures come
running out of the grass-thatched huts. Then he was over
the huts and the plane's shadow was black and racing
across the green waters of the lake and the far line of white
beach danced and shimmered in the heat. A cool beer, he
told himself, and then a bathe. And all with the best
company a man could wish for.

# CHAPTER SEVEN

THEY lay in the shade of a leaning acacia tree, Nina's head resting on his bare, outstretched arm near his wrist so that his fingers could touch and play with the loose blonde hair. And he was thinking that in this situation when they were both drowsy with content it was the oddest damned conversation he had ever listened to. Not a conversation even, not a lazy rising and then dying of phrases and words to mark the happiness they had shared and which still held them. She was talking, lying back with her eyes shut, of the way the Azandes classified diseases.

"They group them in five ways . . . or rather they've been grouped in five ways by Father DeGraer—he was a famous Azande expert. He and Professor Evans-Pritchard. For instance one group is named after the part affected. Like toothache. They call this *Kazarinde. Kaza* is sickness and *rinde* is tooth. And the Azandes think the pain comes from a little maggot gnawing away at the inside of the tooth. Then there's *Kazari.* That's from *Kaza* and *ri* which means head. Then there's *Kazadimo.* That's for backache. *Dimo* means back. Does this interest you, Bill?"

"I'm fascinated."

She laughed softly and turned her head so that for a moment she could bite at the bare flesh of his inner arm.

"I thought you would be. Then there are the diseases which are named after natural things to which they bear some likeness. Epileptic fits for instance. That's *Imawirianya.* It's a lovely word. *Wiri*—small, and *nya*—the red bush monkey. That's because it has certain movements which resemble epileptic symptoms. Though N'Dene tells

me that they also call this *Imagbaru*, sickness of the moth —
that's *gbaru*—because the moth flies into flame at night
just as epileptics during an attack will fall into a fire. One
of the remedies is to eat the ashes of a burnt skull of a red
monkey. Then there are the sicknesses which are named
after their cures. *Imaparabaso*."

"I suffer from that a lot."

"I'm sure you do. It's a stiff neck and the cure is to
move the neck from side to side between two spears. *Para-
baso* means spear-shaft."

"I'll remember that."

He raised himself, leaned over and kissed her full on the
mouth, and her lips held his and her arms closed round
his neck.

When he took his lips from hers she lay with her eyes
still shut and said, "You won't be bored if I go through all
the five groups?"

"I think I shall, frankly. I'll probably get up and
go."

"All right. Then perhaps you'd like to hear about
M'Bori who created the world? In the beginning M'Bori
made everything, fire, earth, water, plants and animals.
And he put the whole lot into an enormous canoe, sealing
them up, except for one hole which he plugged with wax.
Then M'Bori sent for all his sons to come to his great
court. There was the Sun, the Moon, the Night, the Cold
and the Stars and he set them the problem of undoing the
canoe and discovering what was in it. Who do you think
did it?"

"Search me."

"Sun did it. He melted the wax and out poured men,
animals, trees, rivers and hills . . . the whole lot. It's a
nice story, isn't it?"

"It sounds like an African edition of Noah's Ark."

"Yes . . ." Then, her eyes still shut, the sun-dried sand
golden on her arms and legs, she went on, "What do you
do, Bill, when you're not working?"

"What do you mean?" He could still be caught and puzzled by the sudden jumps in her conversation.

"With your spare time. For instance, in the evening, or at the weekend. Do you read much?"

"Only the papers and some technical magazines. I see what you mean. Am I interested in anything apart from flying?"

"Are you?"

"I suppose so. I play golf. I like to go to the theatre when I can. But I'm no intellectual. I'm pretty ordinary."

"No, you're not. Ordinary people go around trying not to be ordinary. Grabbing at things which they hope will change them. You just carry on, don't you, completely content? I like that. It makes you so dependable."

"That's a new word for me."

"It's a good word. Also the other thing I like—" Her eyes opened and she smiled up at him and rolled over on her side, the movement of the long brown body making the dry sand powder from her shoulders, "—is the way you accept things as they come—the pleasant things, that is."

"What about the unpleasant things?"

"You avoid them. Isn't that why you came up to Bisaka?"

"Yes, I suppose it was."

Nina sat up and idly let a handful of sand drift through her fingers.

"What was it?" she asked. "A woman?"

"No."

"I don't believe you." She laughed at his embarrassment. "Was she nice?"

"I tell you—"

"You won't tell me anything you don't want to. Were you in love with her?"

"No."

"Good. Are you in love with me?"

He stood up then and looked down at her, smiling, knowing that he was being deliberately teased. "You ask too many questions. And all the time you know most of the answers. I know how to deal with your kind."

Before she could escape him he bent and put his arms around her, lifting her, and began to carry her down the little beach. She lay in his arms without protest, smiling at him and saying nothing. He waded into the water and dropped her in and then plunged in after her. As they both surfaced some yards out, her face close to his, she said, "Well, that's one way of changing a subject."

\*　　\*　　\*

They had gone to the little island after lunch and it was late in the afternoon when they came paddling back in the rubber dinghy. When they were about a hundred yards off the camp beach Sinclair, who had been paddling mechanically, immersed in his thoughts, heard Nina exclaim behind him, "Oh, Lord—I wonder how long he's been back!"

"Who?" Sinclair turned to her and saw that her face was shadowed with a brief look of concern.

"My step-father." She nodded towards the beach.

Coming down from the camp Sinclair saw two men. One, a tall Azande in khaki shirt and trousers and the other, a white man, short, stocky, wearing breeches and a linen jacket.

"You sound as though you're not glad to see him."

"Don't be ridiculous. Of course I am."

"Who's that with him?"

"Mabenge. He's the big Azande chief around here. He's an educated man."

"You don't like him, either?"

"Bill, shut up!"

"Well, you don't. I can tell from your voice."

As they paddled in slowly, Major Winton came down the beach. He'd obviously seen the Auster, and no doubt

the boys had told him that Nina was out in the dinghy
with the pilot.

They ran the dinghy ashore and Sinclair stepped out and
reached back a hand for Nina. As they turned and made
their first steps up the beach Major Winton came dancing
down to them like a bantam spoiling for a fight. He
halted, gave Sinclair a pugnacious frown, and said, "Who
the devil are you, sir?"

The man's tone was so demanding and rude that for a
moment Sinclair was tempted to reply in the same way,
but he held back his resentment as he felt Nina's hand on
his arm.

"I'm a friend of Nina's. I fly for Voyadis."

"So I see." Winton's head turned briefly towards the
Auster on the far beach strip. "And who gave you permission to come up here? Voyadis knows that I don't like
his planes around here."

Sinclair was roused at once by the man's manner. He
said, holding his resentment down, "Look, I'm sorry. But
this isn't a private estate."

"Maybe not. But planes disturb the birds. Makes my
work twice as difficult, and—"

"Major, please," Nina cut in. "You really are being
impossible. I'm ashamed of you."

Winton's pugnacious face turned towards Nina. "Did
you ask him up here?"

"No, I didn't—but if I'd wanted to I would have done.
What is the matter with you? I really think you should
apologise to Mr. Hadlow."

As Nina finished speaking Sinclair saw Winton's head
jerk upwards.

"Mr. Who?"

"Hadlow. Bill Hadlow," said Sinclair sharply. "And
I'm sorry if I've upset you. I just had a day off and came
up to keep Nina company." He smiled, not caring a damn
about the man. "I don't think the birds minded very
much."

"But this is—" Winton broke off suddenly and turned and looked at Mabenge.

Momentarily, Sinclair got the odd impression that the man had had all the wind taken out of his sails. Mabenge came forward a step, his black face shining, the big body easily held and full of control—a sharp contrast to Winton's impatient bad temper.

Mabenge said calmly, "Miss Nina is right, major. You mustn't be angry with Mr. Hadlow." Mabenge smiled at Sinclair. "We did not get the okapi we went on safari for, Mr. Hadlow. So the major is disappointed. I'm sure you understand, Mr. Hadlow. The birds, too, are very important to the major."

Winton, the effort of mastering himself quite clear, gave a sudden snort. "All right, all right. I apologise. Damn rude of me. I apologise, Mr. Hadlow." He paused for a moment and smiled thinly. "So, you're a new man, eh? How did you get to this part of the world?"

"I just drifted in." Sinclair made it sound pleasant, mostly for Nina's sake, but he still was not liking this man. Who did he think he was to come rushing up like some barking terrier, and then when he was put in order give an insincere wag of his tail which he thought would make everything all right? He sensed, too, that Winton hadn't liked the casualness of his reply. This was a man who asked a question and was used to getting a definite answer. Bad luck for him.

Nina said, "I'll tell you about Bill later, major."

"All right, all right," Winton turned away abruptly and began to walk back towards the camp with Mabenge.

Sinclair, behind his back, raised his eyebrows at Nina. She smiled and gave a little warning shake of her head and whispered, "Don't let him get your back up. He gets these awful moods sometimes."

Sinclair said nothing. He was furious at the way the man had treated Nina. No welcome, no affection for her.

. . . He really needed a hard slapping down, and if Nina hadn't been around he would have got it.

Something of what was in his mind was obviously clear to the girl, for as they walked up the beach behind Mabenge and Winton, she said, "He's not always like this. He can be very nice."

"I'll take your word for it."

She smiled. "Thank you, Bill."

"For what?"

"For taking it so well."

Sinclair grinned. "I don't know why you stick it."

"Because I like it here. I love the Azandes and the animals, and the life here. This lake is right away from the world. It's like a little paradise. Still . . ."

"Still what? Trouble in paradise?"

"Well, yes . . . I must say the major's changed a lot. So much that lately I've been thinking of going."

"Where would you go?"

"I could go to London. All his film and television work is handled there. I could do that for him, or else get some other job."

"London . . . that's a hell of a way." The thought of her going so far dismayed him. "There are plenty of jobs in places like Durban or Nairobi. Why go so far?"

Her eyes, bright and laughing, held his.

"Or Bisaka? Shall I get a job there? Lise Laver would give me one in the hotel. I could keep an eye on you then." For a moment her hand was on his arm, squeezing it.

*     *     *

Later, he saw that if Winton wanted to he could indeed be quite a different person. They all sat under the open grass hut and had an early drink and it was as though Winton had never come fuming down the beach at him. He began to talk about filming animals and Sinclair realised that he was a man of enormous competence in this field. Only once did a touch of the martinet come out and that was when he asked Sinclair what he had done during the war.

"I was with the South African Air Force. Finished up in Italy."

"What were you? Flying Officer . . . Squadron Leader?"

"Nothing so grand. Sergeant Pilot."

Winton grunted and dropped the subject, but there was disapproval at this lack of progress, this want of ambition.

All the time they talked, Mabenge sat a little apart from them, listening but not speaking much, and Sinclair noticed that the Azande chief watched Winton most of the time, almost with a touch of concern.

Just before Sinclair was due to leave, Nina went off to supervise the feeding of their animals and Major Winton went with her. Sinclair was left alone with Mabenge.

When Major Winton was out of earshot, Mabenge said, "I must apologise, Mr. Hadlow, for the way the major behaved. He gets very worked up about things, and he hates to have strangers about his camp."

It sounded odd to have Mabenge apologising for the major, but he did it confidently, without any embarrassment, and Sinclair had the impression of a man of great self containment.

"You've known him a long time?" asked Sinclair.

"Many, many years. He has been here before. All my people like him. In fact," Mabenge smiled, "he has been made my blood brother. This has never happened before in my nation that I can remember."

Before he left Sinclair managed to have a few moments alone with Nina in her tent. He kissed her goodbye, though he sensed that she had one eye open on the tent door in case Winton should show up, and then as he stood apart from her she said, "I won't walk over to the plane with you, Bill."

"Why not?"

"Because the major has said he wants to talk to you alone."

"He's got a hope if he thinks he can stop me from coming to see you. I'll be up again as soon as I can. He'll just have to learn to accept it."

"You're a determined man, aren't you?"

"Only when I know what I want. You really mean that about going to London?"

"I think so."

"I haven't seen London for years. Maybe I'll come along with you."

"But Bill, how could you?"

He grinned. "There could be ways and means."

He moved to her, kissing her again and crushing her to him and while she was in his arms, her mouth and body responding to his caress, he knew that this wasn't like anything he had known before. It bore some resemblance to the usual adult game with its conventional responses and easy little rules . . . but here, both on his side and hers, he could feel that rules and conventions had been thrown aside. It was something he would have to think about, something on which time would have to work. In other words, he told himself as he left the tent, you want to be a bit careful about the whole thing perhaps, otherwise you could be committed. Though come to think of it . . . what was wrong about being committed as long as it was to the right person?

*　　*　　*

Winton walked with him through the gap in the reeds and out on to the long white strip of sand where the plane stood. The mountains were now beginning to throw long shadows over the sand, but it was still hot, with a pearly shimmer of light beating up from the long, hard stretch of lake shore.

Winton said little as they walked, but he chewed at the stem of an empty pipe and kept glancing sideways at Sin-

clair as though he could not make up his mind about
something. Despite the man's apology and his change in
manner, Sinclair knew that between them there still rested
a hard core of dislike. They just weren't the kind, no
matter where or how else they had met, to take to one
another. But he got the feeling that Winton quite deliberately had decided to be nice to him. As nice as he
could be.

Finally as they stood by the plane, Sinclair said, "What's
on your mind, major? If you're not careful you'll bite
that pipe stem in half."

Winton lifted his head and gave a little frown at the
joke, but he took the pipe from his mouth and thrust it
into his pocket.

"It's not easy to say what I want to. Damned difficult
in fact."

"Is it about Nina?"

"Nina? No. Why should it be?"

"Well, you clearly seemed to object to my coming up to
see her."

Winton looked intently at him for a moment, his small
head cocked to one side.

"You fond of her?"

"Yes. I like her."

"Then it's nothing to do with me. Nina lives her
own life. No, it's not that. Though in a way, it affects
that."

"Then what is it?"

Winton hesitated for a moment and then with a curt
little nod said, "Fact is, I want to get something straight
between us. Frankly, I know that your real name can't be
Hadlow. Not Bill Hadlow. Too much of a coincidence."

Sinclair leaned back against the side of the Auster and
reached slowly for a cigarette. Would you believe it?
Here was someone else. First Nahud and now Winton—
he'd obviously picked a false name that was about as useless as it could be. He lit his cigarette and said calmly, "I

think you must say a little more before making an accusation like that."

Winton cleared his throat a little angrily.

"There's nothing much for me to say. Hadlow's flown me in and out of various places on my expeditions. Never been here before, but he was going to fly up here sometime this month to join me. Been expecting him any day. Now you turn up here with his name. Damned odd, to say the least."

Sinclair made his decision. "Well, you're right. I took his name. He was a friend of yours?"

"Yes. A damned good fellow. What's happened to him?"

Sinclair hesitated for a moment, then he said, "I'm sorry to tell you, but he's dead."

"What?" Winton's head came up, chin thrust out like a pugnacious baboon.

"He's dead. I met him after his plane had crashed. He'd smashed up his ribs and he packed up on me the first night. I went through his stuff and seeing the flying licence he had, I decided to take his name in order to get a job in Bisaka. My own licence has been suspended for two years."

"Where was all this?"

"God knows. Miles from here. I went down with malaria the next morning and bumbled about the hills for a couple of days. Next thing I knew I was lying in the hut of old N'Dene at the end of the lake. That's where Nina found me. But didn't she know Hadlow?"

"No. She knew nothing about him. Friend of mine. I didn't even tell her anyone was coming. It was a very loose arrangement between Hadlow and myself. Good God—he's dead. Poor devil."

Sinclair watched him closely. There was something wrong here. Here was Winton who said that Bill Hadlow was a friend of his. A damned decent sort of chap. That wasn't Nahud's description. Not that that mattered much.

Lots of likeable sort of chaps were mixed up in odd affairs.
But there was undoubtedly something odd about Hadlow.
Nahud poking away at his cartridges made that certain.
A warning bell began to ring inside his head.

Nina clearly had known nothing about Hadlow, or she
would have said so right away. But why hadn't Winton
told her a friend of his might be joining them? That was
odd in a place like this where a possible visitor would be a
great matter of interest. And Winton's last exclamations of
regret for the man's death had a perfunctory ring as though
he had thrown them in because they would be expected.

Sinclair said, "Why didn't you tackle me about it when
I was introduced to you?"

"Well, you'd got me on the wrong foot already. Also
I didn't want to embarrass you in front of Nina."

"I see. Did Mabenge know about this man?"

"Yes."

Mabenge had kept pretty cool about it on the beach,
then. In fact he seemed to remember that Mabenge—
when Hadlow's name had been first mentioned—had cut
in on the major, helping him to ride the moment of shock.
No, he didn't like this at all. There was a bad smell to it
somewhere.

Sinclair stirred, walking a few paces from the plane.

"Well, there it is, major. I've taken his name for my
own good—or you may call them bad—reasons. But I
wanted a job flying and it seemed my chance. What are
you going to do about it?"

"Damned if I know. Flying under a false name is your
business. I'm no stickler for regulations much. If Voyadis
or Suchard catch up with you that's your business. But
Bill Hadlow was my friend. Least I can do is to see him
decently buried, not having jackals and vultures pulling
him around. And then there's the plane. That could
possibly be salvaged."

"He was miles from his plane. I never saw that."

"But you could show me where you buried him?"

"Well . . . roughly, I suppose. I was in a bad state myself. Wait a minute. I've got a map in the Auster."

He turned towards the plane. So—here it was, Sinclair thought. Someone else who wanted to know where Hadlow was buried. Well, he could do simple sums. Neither Winton nor Nahud was the least interested in Hadlow as a man. Hadlow had something they both wanted. Well, he wasn't handing anything on a plate to either of them, particularly not to Winton.

He got the map from the Auster and went out to Winton. He spread it out on the tailplane. If he were going to lie it had better be good. He picked an area well away from the cave on the mountain spur.

"Somewhere around there I imagine. There was a little open space just below the tree line, and a big tree, a beobab. I scratched a grave as best as I could under it. I took his passport and his money. . . . Oh, yes, and his rifle and ammunition. I'll let you have them back the next time I come up. But I'll keep the passport if that's all right with you."

"Keep the lot." Winton's voice was almost cordial. "Bill wouldn't have minded. I just want to find him and . . . well, tidy things up. You're sure this is the area?"

"Yes."

"I'll get some Azandes out there right away. You're sure you can't remember any more details of the place?"

"I'm afraid not. I went down with malaria almost immediately afterwards."

"I see." Winton stepped back and Sinclair moved to the plane. He gave a wave of his hand as he climbed in and Winton answered it absently.

A few moments later the plane roared away up the beach, raising a cloud of white sand.

*       *       *

Nina watched the plane take off and then walked along the beach to meet the major. Above her the Auster circled and then disappeared behind the ridge of mountains to the west.

The major came up to her and at once said belligerently, "I don't care for that fellow."

Nina smiled to herself. The major was opening the attack because he knew that she was still annoyed with him. It was a familiar move on his part.

"I like him."

"So it seems. Anyway, I don't care a damn about that. I don't want him encouraged up here—and you know why."

"He doesn't need any encouragement. You really were very rude."

"Well, I've got things on my mind and I can't always stop to be polite. You know what I want to do and it doesn't leave much time for anything else."

She walked beside him now, across the hot sand, and she was aware, not for the first time, but now more acutely than ever, how far they had gone from one another. Although he had never been able to take her real father's place there had been while she was much younger an affection in him for her which she had valued. He, himself, had abandoned this as she got older.

"You know what I think about the things on your mind. I've made a promise to you and that's as far as it goes. But because I've done that it doesn't mean I'm going to stand by and see you being rude to my friends."

"Then don't bring them up here."

"We really have drifted apart, haven't we? I don't think there's much point in my staying here."

He twisted his head round sharply. Then he stopped walking and for a moment put out a hand and touched her on the arm.

"Yes, we have. Why deny it. And I'm sorry. I really wish it could have worked out better. It's my fault, being what I am. But there's no point in crying over spilt milk. You can go whenever you want to."

This, she recognised, was as near an apology as he could ever get. Oddly, in that moment she liked him more than she had ever done, and even felt sympathy for him that outweighed all her disapproval.

She said, "I suppose there's no point in my saying again how wrong I think you are, and how much I wish you would—for your own sake—give up this thing?"

"None at all."

"But why? Why do you want to do it?"

He smiled briefly, beginning to walk on, and said, "Why? Because the thing is there, waiting to be done. So let's say no more about it."

They walked through the cut in the reed bed in silence but when they reached the other side, the camp ahead of them, he said, not looking at her, "You in love with this fellow?"

"I'm not sure. I think maybe I am."

"Well, it's your business, but I'd advise you not to rush into anything you may regret."

Nina laughed. He was hardly the person to give this advice.

"You think he may be a bad hat?"

"Could be. One thing I know. Hadlow isn't his real name."

"How can you know that?" Nina looked at him in surprise.

"No matter. But it isn't his name. He admitted it, too."

Nina knew she would get no more out of him.

Defensively, she said, "That still doesn't make him a bad hat. People change their names sometimes for very good reasons."

He smiled then, and said, "I'm only giving you some advice. Be careful. Though, I imagine I'm wasting my time. If you've fallen in love with him nothing I could say would put you off."

"No, I don't think it could."

He didn't say any more, and neither did she, but she

knew him too well not to realise that his warning note about Bill had not been idly sounded. She would have liked to know what they had talked about at the plane, and she made up her mind that when she met Bill again she would try to find out. A bad hat? Well, it wouldn't surprise her. But it didn't make any difference.

*　　*　　*

Voyadis was waiting for him in the airstrip office when he got back. He was angry about the plane being taken and as he talked, his fly whisk kept smacking up and down on the table. Sinclair let him ease off his head of steam and then said, "All right—so I took a plane without permission. But if you had a girl friend up at the lake you'd have done the same. I'll pay for the petrol. Anyway, why have this rule? Other places one can borrow a plane."

"Not here. Not to go to the lake. Winton doesn't like visitors."

"You're telling me."

Voyadis leaned back and smiled. "I can see you had a row with him."

"I wanted to, but I didn't."

"That was wise. You know, it's a funny thing about small men, they get big ideas. Big men like you—and fat men like me—we may be ambitious, but we are comfortable with ourselves. Not the small men—they're always looking for something. Usually trouble."

"You're a philosopher."

"In a way."

"All I know is—if I'm going to work here I don't fancy the idea of being stuck in Bisaka on my days off. Either I get the use of a plane and run my own risk whether Winton welcomes me at the lake, or I quit."

"Well now . . ." The fly whisk waved gently. "Don't let's be rash about that. After all . . . well, it's a rule I made chiefly because of Laver. He could take her up dead drunk and then where would I be?"

"Then keep the rule for Laver. Not for me."

Voyadis looked at him reflectively for a moment.

"You mean you would quit, if I said no?"

"That's what I mean."

Voyadis heaved himself to his feet.

"O.K. You're a good flier. I don't want to lose you." He smiled broadly. "Besides you're someone new to talk to."

# CHAPTER EIGHT

SINCLAIR did not see Nahud until dinner time that evening. He was halfway through his meal when he came in. Nahud gave him a quick little bob of his head and for a moment hesitated by his table, but Sinclair made no invitation to him to join him. Nahud went across to his own table like a dejected blackbird.

Watching him, Sinclair knew that he was going to have to handle the man carefully. He had made up his mind that he was not going to make any deal with Nahud until he had gone to the grave by himself and had a look round. Already he had worked out a way to do this quickly and, with luck, a way that would not come to the notice of Nahud. Glancing across at his flappy, birdlike movements as he ate, Sinclair wondered whether there was any connection between him and Winton. Both of them were interested in Hadlow's grave. Did they share this interest, or were they on different sides of the fence? Well, whichever way it was, one thing was certain—there was money to be made from his knowledge and, maybe, far more than a hundred pounds.

He finished his coffee and rose from the table. As he went he saw Nahud's eyes come round and follow his movements. He went out of the hotel and down the road past the pilgrim compound. He knew that it would not be long before Nahud followed him. He found a seat on a pile of logs stacked across one end of the small wooden jetty. The moon would be up in another half-hour and already the sky had a faint loom of approaching light in the east. The river slid by, black and silent. Someone was beating a drum in the compound and presently there came the tuneless rise and fall of pilgrims' voices as

they began to sing. There was the shuffling sound of feet
in the dust of the road and Nahud materialised. He stood
in front of Sinclair and gave a nervous cough.

"Mr. Hadlow . . ."

"Hullo, Nahud. You'll get indigestion if you rush your
dinner like that."

Nahud gave a gasping little laugh and settled on a log
a few feet away from Sinclair. "I am anxious to know
what you have decided, Mr. Hadlow."

"I haven't decided anything."

"But I don't understand. I make you an offer. All you
have to do is to accept it—or refuse it."

"It isn't as simple as that, Nahud. It's no good accepting an offer and then not being able to do anything about
it. You know I've been off in a plane today?"

"Yes."

"Well, I wanted to see if I could find the place where
I'd buried Hadlow. If I could have spotted it from the air,
then you could have chartered a plane from Voyadis and
I could have taken you there. But I had no luck. It's as
simple as that."

Nahud stirred uncomfortably. "You really can't remember where it is?"

"That's it. It's a pity. I could have done with a hundred pounds."

Nahud was silent for a while, and then Sinclair saw his
hand go up and fiddle with the row of pen and pencil caps
along his breast pocket.

"It wouldn't be, Mr. Hadlow, would it, that your memory might become sharper if you were going to get more
money? Say a hundred and fifty pounds? Though I
assure you that would be the absolute limit."

"It wouldn't help at all, Nahud. Though, I'll admit
that if I had had any luck I was going to stick out for a
higher price. No, the simple fact is that today I couldn't
find it. But there's no need to be disappointed. As soon
as I can I'll have another look round."

"When will that be?"

"As soon as I can arrange it. I'm a working man, Nahud."

"I see. And assuming you do find it? I have said that a hundred and fifty is my limit. After all this is only a straightforward business of identifying a man."

"Sure. Well, if I can find it, I don't suppose we'll have any trouble over money. Why should we? A hundred and fifty or just possibly two hundred is good money for identifying a man." Sinclair smiled in the darkness as he saw Nahud's arms flap a little as he stood up, as though they were wings helping him to take off.

Nahud came and stood before him. Down on the river bank a few frogs began to tune up, and the drum in the compound thudded away.

With a dry little cough, Nahud said, "Mr. Hadlow, may I speak frankly?"

"Why not?"

"You know exactly where the grave is, don't you?"

"No, I don't. I've told you that."

Nahud shook his head. "I think you do, Mr. Hadlow. And I think also that you have no intention of taking any money from me until you have been there."

"I've no intention of taking any money from you, Nahud, until I can carry out my end of the bargain. That wouldn't be honest, would it?"

Sinclair stood up and patted Nahud on the shoulder comfortingly. "Cheer up, Nahud. I'll keep trying. We'll find the place. After all, there's plenty of time, isn't there? Hadlow can't run away. And all you want to do is to identify him."

They began to walk up the road towards Bisaka, Nahud shuffling along at Sinclair's side, a shapeless, despondent looking figure lost in thought. Although Sinclair was full of curiosity about this man and the anxiety in him to reach the dead Hadlow, he was at the same time touched by an odd sympathy for him. The cares of the world seemed to be on his thin shoulders and he was doing his best not to groan at the weight.

As they approached the entrance to the square, Nahud stopped walking and turned to Sinclair. He made a little fluttering motion of his hands and shook his shoulders inside his over-large suit as though he were cold.

"Mr. Hadlow," he murmured, looking quickly around him, "may I say something, something to which I hope you will not take offence?"

"Go ahead, Nahud."

"It is this, Mr. Hadlow. I hope I am not making a mistake with you. I mean, I hope, that you are not going to become like many other men I have known."

"What's likely to happen to me, Nahud?"

"Without offence, Mr. Hadlow, let us call it greed. In all the world, I do not know what you dream for. Never mind. But, maybe, you imagine you have a chance of getting it now. That could make you unreliable and demanding. You could overstep yourself."

"It's a possibility, I suppose, in any man. Even you, Nahud. What kind of dream, for instance, would make you unreliable and demanding?"

For the first time in their acquaintance Sinclair heard Nahud laugh out loud. It was a high rustling sound, like a sudden squall of wind among bamboos.

"I dream, Mr. Hadlow, of a hundred and fifty feddans of land, outside Khartoum and near the river. It floods each September and when the waters go back it lies dark and smooth like the skin of a young girl. Because I would be rich I would make my brothers work for me. And I would get rid of my present wife and take a young one. It is a wonderful dream and there are times when I have had a chance to make it come true."

"They why didn't you?"

Nahud looked across the square. The hotel lay in shadow and there was a light from its lounge window. Outside the *caserne* a sentry stood, black and still as a statue.

"Because, Mr. Hadlow, I am a man of so little courage that I had no option but to remain honest. You will understand that I am not meaning any offence to you. It is just an explanation. Good night, Mr. Hadlow."

Nahud went shuffling away across the square. Sinclair remained where he was and lit a cigarette, watching him go, feeling a new respect for the man. He was no fool. And if the warning had been vague—and without offence—it had been issued. Nahud knew he was stalling. There was nothing he could do about it. *In all the world, I do not know what you dream for.* He smiled at the memory of Nahud's words. Just for a while Nahud had exposed his real self, let someone else see what was hidden under the shabby, over-sized bazaar suit. A hundred and fifty feddans of land—and a new wife. Well, damn it, he thought, it wasn't an unreasonable demand to make of life.

\*     \*     \*

Sinclair lay on his bed, fully dressed, smoking. Outside the moon had risen and he could see the bone white plaster wall of the barracks and the movement of a couple of scavenging dogs across the grey dust of the square. They quartered about restlessly as though trying to escape from their own elongated shadows.

He looked at his watch. It was a quarter past two.

The moon would last now until dawn almost. He had half an hour's walk to the airstrip from Bisaka. If he left here at half-past two he'd be able to take off just after three. There'd be no one at the airport, except a night-watchman and Amra. By a little after four he could be at the plateau where he had decided a landing could be made. That was going to be the tricky part, making a landing by moonlight. But it could be done. It was the one risky part of the plan. It would take him an hour to the cave and back. No, say two hours. He would be in the air again by six and back at the strip by half-past seven, and into the hotel by eight for breakfast and no one who was going to care a damn would know he had not spent the night in bed.

At half-past two he slid into the corridor. At the far end from the stairs there was a window that faced away from the square with its sentry outside the barracks. The window was already open at the bottom—he had seen to that when he came up to his room. He dropped from it into the hotel garden and made his way between the shrubs and then across country until he met the road a couple of hundreds outside Bisaka. He followed the road, keeping a few yards off it, walking quickly.

At the entrance to the airstrip there was a small grass thatched hut which was used as a check-point for vehicles and people going in and out. There was a high wire fence right round the strip, but the gate by the hut stood open.

He went through, his feet silent in the dust, and slipped around the back of the hut and then, avoiding the road, struck across the burnt-up grass towards the two hangars. The night watchman was probably asleep in the hut at the entrance.

At the back of the first hangar he found the small lean-to in which Amra slept. The boy was curled up on a pile of sacks, his beret slid sideways over his face. Sinclair woke him gently, holding his hand over the lad's mouth as he came out of his sleep. Then when he saw that Amra had recognised him he withdrew his hand. He squatted down by the boy, holding his arm.

"Listen, Amra. You want to do me a big favour?"

"Boss, what you do here this time of night?"

"Amra, listen. You want me to give you proper flying lessons. Make a good flier of you?"

"Yes, boss."

"Then come and help me get the Auster out, and when I take off, you go over to the night watchman and tell him not to worry, not to telephone Mr. Voyadis."

"But what you going to do, boss?" Amra grinned suddenly. "You sure I make good flier, boss?"

"The best. And if the watchman wants to know—you say I'm practising night flying. I'll be back by half-past seven. O.K.?"

"O.K. boss."

They went round the end of the hangar. There was a Dove outside and one of the Austers stood just inside. Between them they could run it out. Sinclair checked the fuel tanks and found them low.

"Fuel, Amra."

They went over to the fuel dump and came back carrying a couple of four gallon cans. They made the trip three times dumping the cans by the side of the plane.

But as they were about to start fuelling the plane Sinclair heard the sound of a car. He straightened up from dumping a can and listened. The noise of the engine roared louder. It was coming up the road to the airstrip. It could be a late lorry going up to the mine, he told himself. But the next moment he knew that he was wrong. A sweep of headlights suddenly scythed low across the flat expanse of runway.

He turned to Amra and gave him a push.

"Get out through the back of the hangar and into your shed. You're asleep and you haven't seen me. Go on. Fast."

Amra, after a moment's hesitation, ran for the back of the hangar. As he disappeared a jeep swung across the front of the hangar, turned sharply and the headlights were full on Sinclair. There was nothing he could do. The jeep ran up to the Dove and stopped, the lights blinding in Sinclair's face.

Four men got out of the jeep and began to walk towards him. He recognised Suchard and close behind him two of his soldiers, armed with carbines, and then as they came closer, the two soldiers fanning out to block the exit from the hangar, he saw Nahud's untidy, flopping figure.

Suchard stopped in front of him.

"Bon soir, monsieur," he said pleasantly.

"Good morning, would be more accurate, I suppose, captain. What brings you up here?"

"Monsieur," said Suchard, "you are under arrest."

For a moment Sinclair said nothing. Then he looked at Nahud who now stood at Suchard's side. Nahud, embarrassed, shuffled his feet.

Sinclair said, "Is this your doing?"

Nahud nodded slowly and half crossed his hands so that he could polish the glass of his wrist-watch with the palm of his right hand.

"I am sorry, Mr. Hadlow," he said gently. "But I did warn you as clearly as I could. It was obvious to me what you might do."

"You're a bright boy, Nahud. But even so—" Sinclair turned to Suchard. "I'd like to know on what charge I'm being arrested."

"Certainly monsieur. You are being arrested for entering the territory of the Central African Republic with a false passport, for operating as a pilot with a false licence, and there are one or two other matters also which I think would be better gone into back at my headquarters."

Captain Suchard stood aside and the two soldiers moved around as Sinclair walked towards the jeep.

# CHAPTER NINE

THE three of them were in Suchard's office. Suchard sat behind his desk, his tunic buttoned although the night was warm. Nahud sat on a chair on the far side of the room, withdrawn into the shadows, his elbows on his knees, his face cupped in his hands. He kept looking at Sinclair with an expression of mixed anxiety and apology, his whole manner uneasy and uncertain, the manner of a man who has taken an irrevocable step and now suffered qualms about his move.

Sinclair, across the desk from Suchard, whatever else he was feeling, meant to give nothing away. There was no anxiety in him, only curiosity. He was not intimidated by authority. Authority for him was only some human being in a uniform. At the moment, too, he was far more interested in Nahud than in Suchard.

Suchard said, "You admit then that you are not Hadlow?"

"I do. I met him on the way up here. He died and I took his papers because they would help me to a job. What's the sentence for using another man's papers?"

Suchard pursed his lips. "I don't know. I shall have to refer to Lassou. Meanwhile you are under arrest and will be detained."

"Can't I be let out on bail?"

"No."

"Isn't that for a magistrate to say?"

"I have the powers to refuse it. You will be kept in custody."

"I see." Sinclair looked across at Nahud. The man's neck shrunk into the collar of his suit protectively, like a tortoise withdrawing. "Why did you do this, Nahud?"

he asked without rancour. He turned to Suchard. "It was Nahud, wasn't it?"

"Yes, it was."

"You know he has offered me money to help him find Hadlow's grave? This seems a funny way to go about things."

Suchard said, "I know all about Nahud's offer to you. Is that what you were going to do when you were arrested? Go off and look for the grave?"

"Of course. I'm a working man. There's a good moon and I should have also had a couple of hours of daylight before getting back to the airstrip. These things have got to be fitted in between jobs."

Nahud stirred, uncupped his face, and said, "Were you going off to find the grave for me, or for yourself, Mr. Hadlow?"

"Sinclair's the name. What else would I be doing? I'd like a hundred and fifty pounds. But you've bitched the whole thing up. I don't get you."

Nahud shook his head slowly. "I think you do."

Sinclair fished for his cigarettes, received a nod of permission from Suchard to smoke, and then said, "It's too late for riddles. I think, Captain Suchard, that I'm entitled to some explanation. First Nahud is prepared to say nothing about my false papers—then he informs on me when I'm trying to help him, and you seem quite content with this. Who is Nahud and what is all this about Hadlow?"

Suchard leaned back in his chair and smiled wryly. Then he looked across at Nahud and said, "I think Sinclair has a right to know. I suggest that you speak for yourself."

The shabby little bundle of over-sized suiting stirred uncomfortably on the chair. A hand shot out and Nahud stared gloomily at his wrist-watch. Sinclair wondered whether the lateness of the night appalled him, or whether he was debating if he could spare the time for explanations.

"Come on Nahud," he said encouragingly. "Out with it. What's the truth about Hadlow?"

Nahud stood up with his hands on the back of his chair, looking rather like a dejected prisoner in the box. He gave a little cough to clear his throat and then, staring over Sinclair's head, avoiding his eyes, said, "You have heard of the Kasai mines in the southern Congo?"

"Yes."

"They are owned by the *Société Internationale Forestière et Minière du Congo*, and they, of course, are tied up with the Diamond Corporation in London. I am only one of the humblest of their employees."

"Cut out the character references and come to the point." But as he said it Sinclair was himself racing ahead to the point . . . diamonds.

"Some weeks ago a parcel of diamonds was stolen from the mines. They were stolen by a trusted native worker in one of the security offices, and handed over then from one man to another." Nahud's eyes met Sinclair's briefly. "I should explain that a large part of the illicit diamond traffic comes north through Khartoum, Cairo and Beirut. Most of it goes to the Iron Curtain countries. The last man to handle these diamonds was Hadlow, who was flying them north."

"So that's it. Hadlow had diamonds on him. Well, I'll be damned. Why couldn't you have said so right out?"

Nahud smiled faintly. "In my business, Mr. Sinclair, we have to be very cautious."

Sinclair gave a short laugh. "And you were! What were these diamonds worth?"

Nahud hesitated, and the pause showed clearly a mixture of respect for the figure he was going to name and embarrassment that he had to name it to Sinclair.

"Around sixty thousand pounds."

"What!" Sinclair sat up sharply on his chair and stubbed his cigarette out in the desk tray. "And you were offering me a miserable hundred quid to get that lot back for your bloody Forestry and Mines outfit? I'll say you're cautious—and damned mean!"

Suchard said, "I must admit it sounds very little for the recovery of such a valuable parcel of diamonds."

"Please, please . . ." Nahud held up a little paw limply. "You must understand the position. If Mr. Sinclair had taken me to the body there was no guarantee that the diamonds would be on it. For that a hundred pounds would have been very adequate. And if they were on Hadlow, I've no doubt my company would have . . . well, been appropriately grateful and would have . . . well, you see my position."

"Like hell I do!" Sinclair made no attempt to hide the anger in his voice.

"I have to do the best I can for my employers."

Sinclair stood up. "Come off it, Nahud. If you could have got that lot back for a hundred quid, you'd have had a big pat on the back, plus a fat commission. A hundred and fifty feddans of land, eh?"

"Please, Mr. Sinclair, that is not so."

Sinclair went over to him, forcing him to look at him squarely. "Well, whether it's so or not—explain another thing. Why did you squeal about my papers? That wasn't going to help you any, unless . . ." He broke off, the whole thing suddenly clear to him, so clear that he had to smile.

"Unless what, Sinclair?" asked Suchard.

"Unless he didn't trust me all of a sudden. He thought that if I found the grave by myself and found the diamonds I would do a moonlight flit with them. Is that so, Nahud?"

Nahud made no attempt to avoid Sinclair's look. "Frankly, yes."·

"Well, that's straight from the shoulder."

"Is it not true?" asked Suchard.

For a moment or two Sinclair said nothing. He looked from Suchard, the man's face uncompromising, neither accusing nor committing, to Nahud who was fidgeting in a quiet agony of perturbation. Was it true? Who could say whether it was true? Until now, he had been content to limit his objectives just to getting to the grave and finding out what all the mystery was about. No, it wasn't true then. But now? Only he knew where the grave was. All the cards were stacked on his side. And waiting for him out there was sixty thousand pounds' worth of diamonds. Nobody could prove a thing for or against him. He could go out to them next week, next month or in five years time and pick them up and—so long as he did the thing discreetly—no one would ever be able to prove that he had taken them. Both men were waiting for him to speak and, catching Nahud's eye, he sensed that Nahud alone realised that this was a moment of decision. There were no flies on Nahud. He was a great little character reader. If he had gone out to the cave and discovered diamonds—then Nahud had put his money on his never coming back. Poor old Nahud—he'd been caught between the devil and the deep blue sea.

"Is it true, Sinclair?" Suchard repeated the question.

Sinclair shrugged his shoulders. "The point doesn't arise. I don't know where the grave is. And I don't think I could ever find it. In fact, all I want to do at this moment is to wash my hands of the whole affair. Just go ahead and refer to Lassou. Find out what my sentence is and I'll serve it. Then I'm out of here as fast as I can go." He sat down and lit a cigarette. As fast as he could go—and he knew exactly where he was going. Nahud would play around with him no longer. The decision was already made in his mind—he meant to have the diamonds.

Suchard stood up and came round his desk. Looking down at Sinclair he said, "I strongly advise you to consider the advantages of complete co-operation with Nahud. I've no doubt that such co-operation will be suitably rewarded by his employers."

"Oh, yes, yes, I'm sure of that," said Nahud eagerly.

Sinclair shook his head. "So far as I'm concerned I've operated on a false passport and flying licence. I'll take what comes for that. These diamonds don't interest me. And there's not a damned thing you can do about it."

Nahud sighed, his shoulders collapsing until his jacket threatened to slip down his arms. "Mr. Sinclair, really . . . you can't expect me to believe that. I am sure you know where the grave is. When you are free you will go on thinking about the diamonds. One day—in a year, in five years—you would try to get them. I know from experience. People have the most curious moral sense about diamonds. You will find the temptation too great. Please think this over."

Sinclair smiled at him. "You want it all ways. First you inform on me because you don't trust me. Now when you've got me safely in clink you read me a moral lecture. Get this straight, Nahud—I'm signing off from the whole affair."

Nahud looked helplessly at Captain Suchard. But he got no sympathy from that quarter. Suchard called through the door to one of the soldiers to come and take Sinclair and, as Sinclair rose, said, "I should have an answer from Lassou in a few days. Until then . . . well you can have your meals sent over from the hotel, and anything else within reason."

"Thank you. I'd like a bottle of whiskey and some soda siphons."

Without a look at Nahud, Sinclair went out with the soldier.

When he had gone Suchard strolled to the window overlooking the inner courtyard. A light shone dimly across the darkness from the men's quarters and a few moths drifted in. Slowly he fitted a cigarette to a long holder and lit it, drawing in the smoke with a deep relish. Then over his shoulder, he said, "I think, Nahud, that one way and another you handled Sinclair very clumsily."

"But captain, what could I do? I was sent down here

on the off chance, merely to keep my eyes and ears open.
A hundred other men went to a hundred other places.
I have little authority and I had to deal with him on my
own initiative."

"It was your intuition, not your initiative that failed.
What now?"

"I must get in touch with my headquarters for a direc-
tive. They can name a reward figure. He will accept a
reward, surely—if it's big enough."

Suchard turned. "I wonder?" he mused. "He is not
the kind of man it is easy to read. I like him, but I do not
deceive myself. . . . He is in a strong position. He could
walk off with those diamonds and—so long as he disposed
of them cleverly—nothing could ever be proved against
him."

"You think he will do that?" asked Nahud mournfully.

Suchard smiled. "I don't let myself think so far. I have
lived too long to presume now to say what men will or will
not do."

Nahud was silent for a moment, then a hopeful smile
illumined his face. "I like him, too. And even though I
mistrusted him . . . you know, I have hopes that he will
accept a reward. Oh, yes, he will accept a reward, of that
I am sure. It is only necessary to keep him here safely until
I can name a figure."

Suchard flicked the ash from the end of his cigarette.
He said nothing, but his eyes were steadily on Nahud,
and slowly the hopeful smile faded from Nahud's face.

"But surely, captain . . . if the reward is big enough?"

Suchard shook his head. "What reward will be big
enough, as big as sixty thousand pounds? You are in
competition, Nahud, with a powerful outside bidder.
Good night."

\*       \*       \*

The cell was in a low-roofed run of buildings that
abutted on to the main headquarters. The only door to it

opened through the main orderly room of the barracks.
There was one barred window on the square side, set at
about chest height so that a prisoner could stand and
watch the slow progression of Bisaka life. There was nothing to stop a prisoner's friends gathering outside and talking to him. It was a pleasant, friendly arrangement. The
room had a table, a chair, an empty tin bowl, and a
wooden bunk bed built against the wall opposite the window. A man could lie on his bed even and talk with his
friends outside.

Sinclair lay on his bed, watching the light against the
barred window paling towards dawn. So, Hadlow had
been carrying diamonds. But he was the only man who
knew where Hadlow was. He knew, but nobody could
prove whether he knew or not. The thing was an absolute
gift. The moment he could get free he quietly took them.
It was the chance of a lifetime. So long as he was careful
in disposing of them no one could ever prove that he had
them. He'd be a fool to turn down a chance like this. He
wasn't so stupid that he wouldn't admit that there was a
moral issue involved. But it wasn't one that worried him.
This wasn't like robbing a bank. Here were a lot of
diamonds that—but for him—could have been lost for
ever. He didn't care a damn about the diamond company.
They had a monopoly of diamond digging in this country
that was almost feudal.

He lit a cigarette. As far as he was concerned everything
was quite clear. It just wasn't in his nature to miss this
opportunity. The whole thing was a challenge, and he was
the type who had to take a challenge. The fact that a
vague body like the *Société Internationale Forestière et
Minière du Congo* were going to be sixty thousand pounds
down didn't bring any tears to his eyes. They'd still pay
the same dividend.

Suddenly a thought made him sit up. He had overlooked Winton's interest in the matter. Winton for sure
must know about the diamonds. That meant he hadn't

got all the time in the world. There was no knowing when some wandering Azande hunter might not poke his nose into that cave and find Hadlow. Mabenge would be told and the diamonds would be lost. Yes, the sooner he got moving the better. He reached over and stubbed his cigarette out on the floor. Tomorrow, he would be at the window and find someone to get Amra down to him. The next time he went up to the airstrip he did not want to have to fiddle around fuelling up an Auster.

\*   \*   \*

As Mabenge walked along the lakeside, the first rays of the morning sun tipped the far mountains and touched the waters of the lake. He stopped, feeling the sun suddenly warm on his bare torso, and watched the slow movement of the morning flight of the flamingoes begin. In a few moments the air was thick with them and he waited for the magical second when the haphazard, criss-crossing flight turned into the long, lazy, superbly drilled circling with every bird flying in sympathy with the black flamingo at the head of the rising, wheeling cloud. He watched, delighted; watched as an Azande, an Azande prince, for whom the black bird had traditional significance, his emotions native, springing from his heritage; and he watched, too, even on this morning when he was deliberately removing himself from its influence, as a European-educated man, a man of reason and logic. He was well aware of the two natures within him; the black Azande prince, and the London University educated Bachelor of Economics.

He threw his head back, straining his neck, keeping his eyes on the black flamingo, and he freely acknowledged with one part of his mind the mystery and magic of his tribe's beliefs, while with some other part he understood the impatience Winton so often showed towards his superstition. Though Winton would never deride his beliefs, Mabenge was aware that he felt he should have outgrown them. But how could a man outgrow, or out-educate the influences and blood bonds of his birth? He was an Azande first, a Western educated man second. This gave him a foot in each camp. But when he was troubled, he returned always to the camp of his birth. It was as much compulsive in him to consult the poison oracle as it was compulsive in a European to touch wood, to avoid walking under ladders, or to throw spilt salt over a shoulder. He smiled to himself. The white people might not consult the oracles when they began a project, started a journey, found themselves in doubt or wished to know whether a venture would be successful, but nevertheless they had their lucky days, their stars, and their counsellors.

He walked on, along the lake shore, wearing only a *roka* around his loins. N'Dene would have been offended if he wore any European clothes. The *benge*, the poison used in the oracle making, was sensitive to many outside influences. Mabenge could remember the stories his father had told him of the collecting of *benge*. It was made from a poisonous creeper which did not grow north of the Uelle-Kibali river and was chiefly found in the region of the Bomokandi river. For the widespread Azande nation the collection of *benge* meant long and difficult journeys, and from the start of the trip the picked men who made the journey had to observe strict taboos so that the poison would not be polluted. No man, while the expedition lasted, must have sexual relations with a woman, nor must he eat fish or elephant flesh, or smoke hemp, and the eating of certain plants was forbidden. Sexual intercourse with a boy was permissible for it was well known that a boy did not pollute the oracle. And when the *benge* was collected and brought back it had to be kept free of pollution, and Mabenge knew that N'Dene would keep his *benge* well away from the homestead hidden in a hole in a tree or under a bush.

He saw N'Dene waiting for him on the lakeside below the homestead. N'Dene had his grandson with him and the boy was carrying a grass basket in which were the young fowls that would be used in the oracle making. In the old days when a prince such as Mabenge consulted the oracle it was always operated by a young boy under the control of an elder like N'Dene, and when the oracle was over the young boy was slaughtered so that none of the prince's secrets should become known. But time and the coming of the white men to Africa had changed that. Today the boy would leave them at the edge of the bush and N'Dene would operate the oracle.

N'Dene gave him a greeting and they walked on by the lake to a point where thick trees and shrubs reached right down to the water. Here Mabenge took the basket of fowls from the boy and the two men went on into the bush. Always the oracle had to be operated in shade, away from the sun. The morning was the best time and it was never done on the day after a new moon.

They found a small clearing in the bush and they both squatted down on the grass, about ten feet apart, and as they sat down they were both careful to tighten and spread out their *rokas* for no man must expose himself before the *benge*. It must be given the same respect as one gave to one's parents. But while N'Dene began the preparation they spoke to one another in low voices about ordinary things for apart from its magic, the oracle consultation was also a social event. In the old days a consultation could involve a dozen or more people, all wishing to put questions, and could last for many hours.

N'Dene, working away, told Mabenge how in the old days he had used to go and collect *benge*, how the roots were dug up, cleaned, and then scraped to a red powder which was placed in the sun for three days to dry, and how when the time came for carrying it back home this was done in baskets lined with banana leaves and how the baskets were always carried on the shoulder, never the head, for this would cause all a man's hair to fall out. As he was speaking N'Dene poured some water from a gourd on to the *benge* which he had placed on a large leaf. Mabenge saw the poison effervesce slightly and then N'Dene began to mix it into a paste with his fingers. With a twig he took some of the paste and put it on a smaller leaf which he rolled up, funnel-shape, so that he could squeeze the leaf and let the poison liquid from the paste drip from one end into a fowl's beak. This done he pulled the basket of fowls to him and took out a bird.

He put the bird on the ground on its back, his left foot holding it by one wing and its legs, the bird's head facing him.

N'Dene looked at Mabenge and said, "The *benge* is old. It may be impotent like an old man, or in age have become stupid and hot to kill."

Mabenge nodded. He knew what N'Dene meant. The whole point of the oracle was that some fowls would die and some live. If the poison was hot and stupid it would kill all the fowls. If it were impotent none of the fowls would die. In either case the *benge* would be useless. First of all the *benge* had to be tested and this must be done with some unimportant set of questions. The way of putting the questions was important, too, for the answer to the first question had to be corroborated by the answer to the second.

"Begin, O N'Dene," said Mabenge. His first 15 questions would be simple ones to test the *benge*.

N'Dene took his small leaf filter and, holding the fowl's head with his left hand, he opened its beak and with his right hand squeezed a few drops of the poison liquid from the paste into its throat. He closed the fowl's beak and shook its head to make it swallow the liquid.

Mabenge said, using the proper formulae, "Poison oracle, poison oracle, you are in the belly of the fowl. If the white man Hadlow be truly dead, kill the fowl. But if the white man Hadlow be alive, spare the fowl."

N'Dene lifted the fowl in both hands, shook it gently and then sat it on the ground. The bird stood motionless for a few seconds, then suddenly it began to stretch and close its wings spasmodically. Its head and neck were raised stiffly, the beak wide open. It took a few paces forward and then collapsed, dead, on the ground.

Mabenge nodded approvingly. Hadlow was truly dead. But the fowl's death might only mean at the moment that the *benge* was too hot and would stupidly kill every fowl.

N'Dene reached for another fowl, imprisoning it with his left foot, and then administered poison to it.

Mabenge said, "Poison oracle, poison oracle, you are in the belly of the fowl. You have said that the white man Hadlow is dead. If this be true, spare this fowl."

N'Dene raised the bird and shook it, violently this time, to give the *benge* every chance to prove that it was too hot. He placed the bird on the ground and both men watched it carefully. That this fowl lived was important to prove that the *benge* was good *benge*. The poison had passed the first test, the *bambata sima*, now it must pass the second, the *gingo* to prove its worth. The fowl shook its head, ruffled out its wing feathers and then walked quietly across the clearing, pecking at the ground. From one of its legs trailed a length of creeper which N'Dene's grandson had tied to its leg. The fowls that lived the boy would later have to collect from the bush where they had strayed and it was easy to catch a fowl with a creeper tied to its leg.

"It lives," said N'Dene. "It is good *benge*." He took another fowl from the basket and held it on the ground with his foot. Then looking at Mabenge he said, "You have many questions, O Mabenge? Questions that the white major cannot answer?"

Mabenge's face showed nothing. But inwardly he was smiling at N'Dene's jealousy of the major. N'Dene loved and respected him and did not approve of his friendship with the major.

"Only two questions, N'Dene. It is good *benge*. You have kept it well."

N'Dene grunted and began to administer poison to the

third fowl, and when it was done Mabenge said, "Poison oracle, poison oracle, you are now in the belly of that fowl. Listen well, poison oracle. On the body of the dead white man are many diamonds. If these diamonds will come into my hands, kill the fowl. But if these diamonds will never come into my hands, spare the fowl."

N'Dene raised the fowl and shook it and then placed it on the ground. Almost before its feet touched the grass it fell over on to its side in a fierce convulsion, beak gaping wide, and was dead.

Mabenge's face showed no elation. This was only the *bambata sima*. The *gingo* was still to come.

N'Dene took another fowl and prepared it.

Mabenge addressed the *benge*. "Poison oracle, poison oracle you are now in the belly of that fowl. You have said that the diamonds will come into my hands. If that be true, spare the fowl."

N'Dene shook the fowl and set it on the ground. The bird stood for some time motionless, then shook its head a little and began to move across the clearing, flicking one leg impatiently because of the creeper length attached to it.

"It lives," said N'Dene.

Mabenge nodded. The diamonds would come to him. That was enough. Not for one moment, now, did he doubt the truth of the oracle. He was all Azande and the oracle had spoken. He was well content.

N'Dene had prepared another fowl and was holding it up in his hands.

Mabenge said, "Poison oracle, poison oracle, you are now in the belly of that fowl. The black flamingo flies over the lake and the others follow his flight each morning. Say then, if the morning is coming when the black flamingo will lead the others from the lake far to the south and the sky will be dark with the Azande birds, spare the fowl. But if that flight will never come—kill the fowl."

N'Dene placed the fowl on the ground and it lived.

But when Mabenge put the *gingo*, "Poison oracle, poison oracle, you have said that the black flamingo will fly south leading the others—if this be true, kill the fowl," the fowl that was put on the ground did not die. After a little while it wandered off into the bush to join the others.

N'Dene said, "The oracle will not answer. Maybe it will not answer today because it is tired. But maybe it will never answer, O Mabenge, for there are some things which rest with M'Bori alone and he does not reveal them to men until the time comes."

"True, N'Dene, but I am content with what has been said."

N'Dene began to pack up his poison into a little grass basket he had brought with him and he gave a shout for his grandson to join them and collect the fowls. Soon the bush was noisy with the clucking of the birds as the small boy chased after them.

As N'Dene and Mabenge walked back to the lake, N'Dene chatted quietly with his prince. There were many things he knew, but many more he wished to know from Mabenge, but on some matters Mabenge was always guarded and this N'Dene resented but had to accept. He knew, for instance, that all the spare Azandes had gone off with the major to look for the grave of the white man. But he was confused in his mind about this white man for he thought that the white man referred to was the one he had treated in his hut. Mabenge explained to him that there had been two white men, and one had buried the other and taken his name.

"It is the grave of the dead man we look for now, N'Dene. But the white man who has taken another's name cannot remember exactly where the grave was."

"If a man buries another how can he forget where the grave is?" asked N'Dene.

Mabenge smiled. "An Azande would not forget, N'Dene, because to us the forest and mountains are familiar things. But to some white men they are just a confusion. But the grave will be found. It has been said."

N'Dene did not reply. He was thinking of the way he and his grandson had found the sick man on the mountains. From Mabenge he knew that the white man had only travelled two days' journey from the grave at that time, and in his sickness he could not have travelled far. Suddenly, because of what the oracle had said, and because his jealousy made him seek always to rival the white major, he longed to be the one to find the grave. He could find it perhaps and show Mabenge how much more useful he was to him than the white major. He looked up from the lakeside towards the mountain crests. It had been up there that they had found the white man. He was an old man and travelled slowly. But the boy could come with him and carry his pipe and tobacco and the little food they would need. Old men travelled slowly, maybe, but in their wisdom and experience they travelled surely. A young man would turn aside for a woman in the bush, or to seek the honey from a bees' nest, and when he arrived he would find the old man already there.

# CHAPTER TEN

H E had never been in jail before and, if he ever went into one again, he had a feeling that it would certainly not be as sociable and comfortable as this one.

His food was brought over on a tray from the Bomu hotel by Lise, who was amused by the situation and not a little curious.

"No one will say why you're here, Bill. But there are all sorts of rumours."

"The whole thing is a mistake."

"Yes? I should think that's what all prisoners say."

"Well, it's what I'm saying."

"I see. You're going to be as clammy about it as Suchard and that Hussein Nahud."

"That's it."

"Well, it's none of my business, but if you want a file smuggled in I might arrange it."

Sinclair grinned. "No need. I've looked at the window. The bars are just set in the wooden frame and the frame's full of dry rot. I'd only have to push hard against the thing."

Although she laughed, he, himself, was quite serious about it. The frame was indeed rotten and he meant to go out that way.

Most of the day he stood by the window receiving visitors. Pete came and had a chat with him and was just as curious as Lise. And later Voyadis paid a visit and wanted to know if he could make arrangements with Suchard to bail him out.

"Don't try. He won't wear it."

"But what have you done?"

"Nothing very much. I'll be out soon, but I think

you'll have to write me off as a flyer. Pity, I liked the job."

The one person he wanted to see was Amra, and it was late afternoon before he saw the familiar red beret and green pullover coming across the square. He called to Amra and the boy came up to him grinning.

"What you done, boss?"

"Nothing, Amra—except that Captain Suchard doesn't want me flying round here any more."

"He think you bad flier?"

"Could be."

"That soldier is crazy. What you want me to do, boss?"

"What makes you think I want anything done?"

Amra grinned. "If I was in jail, boss, and my girl friend was long way away, I'd want to go and see her."

"Well, that could be, Amra. So what do you suggest?"

Amra pushed his beret to one side and scratched his head.

"I'll see the Auster is ready, boss. Also, I leave my bicycle round the corner of the hotel tonight for you. But how you get out?"

Sinclair tapped the wooden window frame. "Push my way out. And Amra, you have that Auster ready—but don't hang around there. You get right out of the way—in case there's trouble. Understand?"

Amra grinned and nodded. Then putting his hand into his pocket he pulled out a hunting knife and slipped it quickly through the window to Sinclair. With a quick glance round the square, he said, "You don't bother with this window, boss. Them bars will fall out and the sentry will hear. My father help build this place. The roof's flat, just plaster and some lathes, boss. You stand on your table and cut your way out. That's what my father say. He ever in jail, stand on the table and cut his way out. Nobody hear you, nobody see you. O.K. boss?"

"O.K. Amra. I'll leave something for you in your shed. But you keep away tonight, eh?"

"O.K. boss."

When Amra was gone he had a look at the ceiling. Standing on his table he found he could push the point of the knife right through the plaster.

Just before sunset Nahud paid him a visit, but it was not the informal type through the window from the square. He was let into the cell by one of Suchard's men and locked in with Sinclair.

He sat down on the end of the bed with a quick little ruffle of his shabby suit and his whole manner suggested a weary sigh.

"Captain Suchard," he said, "flies down to Lassou to-morrow. When he comes back in the evening, he will have instructions about you."

"Good—the sooner I get out of here the better. Damn it all, I've only used a false passport. That's no great crime."

"I agree. You may be released. Deported that is. Or detained here longer. From Lassou Captain Suchard will be sending a cable to my employers in Khartoum and should have an answer before he comes back. I am asking them to name a positive reward figure, Mr. Sinclair, for the return of the diamonds. And I have urged them to be generous."

"So?"

"As a personal favour, I ask you to do nothing rash until we have an answer."

Sinclair shook his head. "Listen, Nahud, your people have got nothing to offer—because I've got nothing to give. I'm fed up with this whole business. Somewhere out in the wilds is a man with diamonds on him. Let him stay there. I'm just shaking the dust of this place from my feet as soon as possible. That's the position. Nobody can make me say where Hadlow is if I don't know."

"You know perfectly well, Mr. Sinclair."

"Nobody can say that and be certain. Let him rest."

Nahud gave a gentle shake of his head. "I wonder why

it is that when diamonds are concerned most people seem to lose all their scruples."

"Fascinating subject, Nahud. Here's another for you, too. Bit of a headache attached to it. Haven't you overlooked the fact that Hadlow, presumably, was only a carrier of diamonds for other people. Those other people are around somewhere."

Nahud's head came up with a jerk and his hand went nervously to his pens and pencils. Sinclair smiled, but the answer was quite unexpected.

"That's interesting, Mr. Sinclair. I've never brought that point up before, because I was wondering how long it would be before you mentioned it. Of course I realise that there were other people behind Hadlow. Do I presume that an approach has already been made to you? Don't bother to answer because I know it won't help me." He stood up and curiously he suddenly seemed more certain of himself, as though some point which had been worrying him was now cleared. He turned and put his hand on the window sill. "By the way, Captain Suchard is well aware of the insecurity of this cell. At my suggestion, which annoyed him a little though he saw its good sense, he is putting a man specially on guard outside this window all night."

"Oh, is he?" Sinclair made his voice angry, though there was no anger in him. "Then blast you for an efficient busybody."

Nahud smiled broadly. "I am only doing my job, Mr. Sinclair."

When he was gone Sinclair realised that he had to work fast. Suchard's sentry would come on duty when darkness fell. It would be difficult to work at the ceiling without making a noise. He decided to begin right away. He pulled the small table over into a corner where it could not be seen outside in the square. Anyone coming in through the orderly room would give him warning with the fiddling and scraping with lock and bolts. He already had had his evening meal so no one was likely to visit him again that evening.

He stood on the table and began to prise and cut away at the plaster with his knife. Luckily for him it was dry and thin and came away from the lathes in great irregularly shaped slabs. He gathered these slabs carefully as they came loose and hid them away under the blankets of his bed. Within half an hour of Nahud's leaving he had cleared a space a couple of feet square in the corner of the ceiling. All he had to do when the moment came was to cut through the lathes and with his hands push the outside plaster upwards. It would make some noise, but done carefully he hoped that the sentry would not be aroused.

The preliminary work done he went and sat on his bed and fixed himself a whiskey and soda to take the taste of plaster dust from his mouth. He smiled to himself. So that was Nahud's secret worry. That some other party had made him an offer which, in the nature of things, would be bigger than anything Nahud's employers would offer. Quite clearly they wouldn't pay a penny more than they were forced to pay. Why should they, they probably said? Expenses must be kept down and profits up. He fixed himself another whiskey and went to the window to watch the evening square.

The lights were on in the Bomu hotel. There was probably a bridge game going on. Henri Toubbu was back from a pilgrim run because he had seen the returning pilgrims filing across the square just before sunset. Henri would take his place in the four.

The air was hot and still and the bats were out, hawking across the lighted front of the hotel. Some coloured boys were squatting on the far side of the square in the dust playing some native gambling game with small sticks. A woman went by carrying a basket on her head, walking with the grace of the Queen of Sheba. For a moment the whites of her eyes flashed curiously towards him at the window. Then a little later the sentry came on duty. He came right up to the window and gave Sinclair a smiling nod of the head. He was young, coloured, but not an Azande. Probably from one of the tribes lower down the Congo. Africa, a new world, and with a new people inheriting their world for the first time, thought Sinclair. By God, they had a plateful in front of them. But given time they would make a go of it. He was sure of that. They were all good and simple people. That was the trouble at the moment, they were too good and too simple to see what their leaders were doing with them. But they would learn.

He said to the sentry, "When I go to sleep, boy—don't you go tramping and clanking about right outside. When I'm ready to bust out these bars I'll give you a shout."

The sentry grinned. "Yes, captain—you shout loud. I come." He looked at the glass in Sinclair's hand. "They never give me no whiskey when I was in there."

"I'm an important prisoner. They've got to keep me friendly. I'll leave the bottle for you when I break out."

"Yes, captain. You do that for certainly. Then I get drunk and lose this stripe which I just got back. Always I keep getting a stripe, then getting drunk and losing it, and then getting it back. I don't seem to get beyond one stripe somehow."

Sinclair went back to his bed and lay down. It was damned uncomfortable on top of the hidden plaster. Pity about the sentry. He was going to lose his stripe again if the breakout went off successfully.

\*　　\*　　\*

In the end old N'Dene had not taken his grandson with him. The boy's mother, the most shrewish of N'Dene's many daughters, had said that he was too young to spend days and nights on the mountain with an old man whose mind was beginning to wander. She had said this to N'Dene's face down by the lake, and N'Dene had shook with anger at the disrespect this woman was showing him. Unfortunately her husband was away with Major Winton looking for the white man's grave so he could not be called upon to give her a beating and N'Dene himself had not the strength. But she should be beaten, he promised himself, when her husband returned.

In the end he had gone off by himself just before sunset. The poison oracle had said that the diamonds would come into Mabenge's hands. N'Dene had found the white man who had buried the diamond carrier, found him, nursed him, and because of this he felt that only he could find the grave. But even so, he had to be sure. He was too old a man to wander for days on the hills if right from the start it had been decided that he should not find the grave. A true Azande did not take a wife, begin a journey, make any decision without first consulting the oracle. Not the poison oracle, for that was reserved for matters of great moment and was never used, for instance, by women. There were always the other oracles; some so simple that a child or a woman could work them, like the stick oracle. N'Dene had debated whether he should put his question to the rubbing board oracle or to the termite oracle. In the end he had decided on the termite oracle, chiefly because he liked the taste of termites and also because it would take him away from the homestead that night and so put out of his sight and mind his daughter and her disrespect for him. It had taken a long time for the memory of that to ease in his mind. He had grumbled to himself all the way up from the lake, following the line of a small feeder stream which was marked with a matted growth of bushes and trees. But even though he had grumbled and been angry his eyes had been alert, searching. Some way up the stream he had found what he wanted, a clump of shrubs hanging over the water. He had cut a small branch from a *dakpa* shrub and another branch from a *kpoigo* bush, long, slender stems, regularly leafed. Carrying them carefully he had worked his way up the hill, high above the homestead, the light fast dying in the sky, to the place of the termite mounds which was not far from the

spot where he had found the sick white man. Just before
the sun had sunk he had halted at the largest mound and
clambered stiffly to the top. With his hands he had
scraped away until he had exposed one of the big tunnels
used by the blind termites. Then, holding the branches,
one in each hand, he had raised his eyes to the darkening
sky and had intoned to the termites, "The mountains are
before my eyes, O oracle. If I am to find the white man's
grave, then eat thou the *kpoigo* branch. But if I am not to
find it, then eat thou the *dakpa* branch."

He had then inserted both branches into the tunnel and
had closed the top. This done he had sat down at the foot
of the mound and had prepared to pass the night, waiting,
for the branches must not be uncovered until the first
light of the morning sun.

He sat there now with an old blanket over his shoulders,
shivering and grumbling to himself. Occasionally his
mind wandered in the way an old man's mind will. But
always it came back to the thought of the diamonds.
Major Winton and a party of men had gone off to find
the grave. They had gone off chasing the tails of the ones
ahead like a pack of monkeys. And going where? To
some spot under a beobab tree which, Mabenge had said,
the sick white man had said was the place of the grave.
They were all fools. What white man would tell others the
place of hidden diamonds? The white men had a madness for diamonds and they would not help others to them.
Clearly the sick white man would come back for the diamonds. But he, N'Dene, would find them first. It would
be a good thing to show Mabenge that his wisdom was
greater than the wisdom of Major Winton. Mabenge
loved this white major too well. Had even made him his
blood brother. N'Dene, spat angrily at the thought. Then
the anger went and pleasure took its place at the thought
that Mabenge had come to him for the poison oracle.
Mabenge was a prince and the poison oracle of a prince
was of great importance. It was a pity that these days it

could not be worked as it had in the days of old King Gbudwe. In those days only young boys and youths handled the fowls, while men like himself would do the questioning for the king or prince, and the king or prince would sit by smoking and drinking beer, and when the oracle was done the young boy would be killed so that the great secrets and their answers would not be told. He had heard even that in the far kingdom of Ndoruma, the son of King Ezo, the youths had had their testicles crushed with blows of hammers so that of a certainty they would be unpolluted when they came to handle the fowls. But all that was passed away for some strange reason. The white men, who themselves loved killing and torture, had forbidden it. The white missionaries, who fortunately came seldom to this part of the land, were more intolerant than the others for they forbade the oracles. How strange were the white men. Then remembering Major Winton and Mabenge's love for him, he spat angrily.

\*          \*          \*

For all his friendliness the sentry was no fool to be lulled into laziness by companionable words. Until midnight he patrolled regularly up and down outside the window and Sinclair, lying on his bed, could see the blackness of the frame blackened more as the man's face turned and he peered inside. Obviously the sentry valued his stripe. Getting drunk was something that he could not help. The bottle was there and his hand went out and the stripe was lost. But he had no intention of losing it by letting a prisoner slip from him.

Sinclair was patient. He had time on his side. So long as he arrived at the airstrip just before dawn then he would be content. The sentry was doing an all-night tour for Suchard had few men. Towards dawn he anticipated that the sentry would tire. His patrols would be less frequent and for a certainty he would squat down with his back to the cell wall. It was for this that Sinclair waited.

It came about four o'clock. Uncomfortable though his bed was with its packing of plaster, he had had to fight the desire to sleep in himself. But at four he heard the unmistakable sound of a snore, faint, but definite, from outside. He slid off the bed in his stockinged feet and went to the window. By craning his neck he could see, a few yards away to the left, the legs of the sentry flat on the ground. Another gentle snore hissed and then faded with a sleepy grunt.

Sinclair went back to his bed, picked up his shoes and, tying them together, hung them round his neck.

He climbed on to the table and began to work at the lathes. He had thought he might have trouble with them, but most of them were rotten and eaten by ants or termites and crumbled over his head, spilling dust on him. Within ten minutes he was through to the night sky, seeing the stars brilliant above him. Carefully he pushed at the edges of the hole, working the loose plaster up and outwards on to the roof. When the hole was big enough to take him he got the cell stool and stood that on the table.

He worked himself out of the hole, reaching forward, and then rolled gently to free his legs, anxious at the thought of the weakened roof collapsing under him. One piece of plaster from the inside ceiling did fall with a clatter on to the table. He lay on the roof, his feet still over the hole, waiting to see if the sentry had been roused. There was no sound from the square.

A few moments later, he was lowering himself from the flat roof on the far side of the cell and out of sight of the sentry. He went away then, up the side of the square, keeping in the shadows, silent in his shoeless feet, and crossed the road to the airstrip a hundred yards above the square. Plaster dust had worked down inside his shirt and he pulled the tails of his shirt out over his trousers to free it from his body. He came back towards the square, keeping well away from the road and, after a little trouble, found Amra's bicycle propped against a shed at the back of the hotel. He picked it up and slung it on to his shoulders and headed across the dusty, grassless waste ground behind the hotel towards the airstrip road. Three minutes later and he was cycling easily up the road, wondering what the reaction of the sentry would be when he woke and resumed his patrolling. He had left half a bottle of whiskey standing on the window sill for him. Now he could get drunk and lose his stripe the normal way.

This time, not knowing what precautions Nahud might have persuaded Captain Suchard to take at the airstrip, he did not go as far as the main gate. When he hit the first length of netting that enclosed the field, he dismounted, propped the bicycle against the fence and then, standing on the saddle, jumped over the top.

Two hundred yards away, black against the moon and starlit night, the bulk of the two hangars rose hard and sharp. Crouched low he went across the open ground and gained the shadow of the first hangar. Here he waited for a while, listening. If Suchard had a patrol on the field they must make some noise. But there was no sound from the hangars.

He went round to the back of the first hangar and found Amra's shed. It was empty and he dropped a couple of twenty dollar bills on to the pile of sacks which was Amra's bed.

A few moments later he was at the top end of the hangar. Twenty yards from him one of the Austers stood out in the moonlight, facing towards the runway. All he had to do was to get into it, press the button and go. And at the moment he was not thinking any farther ahead than that.

He waited, looking round towards the main gate and the watchman's hut. There was no sign of life anywhere except for a large white owl that came drifting like a ghost low to the ground and went by him with a soft beat of wings.

He walked out into the moonlight, not hurrying, and in ten yards was in the shadow of the plane. The cockpit door was open and he got in.

The propeller turned with a stiff, almost awkward re-
luctance for a second or two as the battery ground away
and then, with a burst of sound that split the peace of the
night into fragments, the motor roared. He did not wait
for any warming up. He gunned her away and up towards
the runway and, with his eyes on the far end of the field,
delayed until the last moment the lift that would take her
up, airborne, free, making him master of his own actions.
He saw the sky was beginning to pale with the coming
dawn. He could not have timed it better.

He lifted her and she slid from the ground, putting her
nose up gently as though sniffing at the night air. Then
the grey-coloured earth was sliding obliquely below him
as he began to bank and turn and the first long black
sinuous coil of the Bomu shook itself from the trees.

He brought her right round, racing at five hundred feet in
a wide circle and, for the hell of it, came down over Bisaka.
As he swept over the square he saw a single figure run out
on to the moonlit dust and a pair of arms reach up towards
him. Then he was over and heading north up the river,
smiling to himself and reaching in his pocket for a cigarette.

As he put it in his mouth there was a movement from
behind him. A bare brown arm came over his shoulder
and a cigarette lighter was snapped under his nose. He
did not turn. A happy grunting sound told him all he
wanted to know.

"Amra," he said out of the corner of his mouth, "I
ought to beat the skin off your arse for this."

"Yes, boss. You mind if I smoke, too, boss?"

"O.K. But you've missed yourself forty dollars I left in
your shed."

"Who wants money, boss? I say to myself—Boss, he
break jail—he can't come back. So that suits me. Time I
was taking off for myself, boss. O.K. boss?"

"I hope so. We'll think about it later."

Behind him Amra began to chuckle and grunt with the
pleasure of it all.

# CHAPTER ELEVEN

As soon as the first rays of the sun tipped the mountain crests N'Dene rose from the ground and walked stiffly away from the termite mounds to the small stream. He was cold and shivering, but soon the strengthening sun would warm him. He washed his hands and face and then cupped water into his mouth with his hands, rinsing it around inside his mouth and blowing it out with great force. When he felt that he was clean of the night's discomforts and dirt he went back to the termite mound and began to uncover the tunnel into which he had thrust the branches.

The *kpoigo* branch had been stripped bare of all its leaves, but the *dakpa* branch remained untouched. The oracle had declared itself. He was to find the grave of the white man. There was no elation in him. The oracle had confirmed what he knew must be. Back by the stream he carefully wrapped both branches into a large leaf and put them into the bag which held his few provisions for the journey. A man must carry with him the oracle branches when he travelled. He was in no hurry. The thing was to be.

He waited for the sun to strengthen and rise, waiting to see the distant flight of the flamingoes before he started. As he stood on the hillside, away to the south he thought he heard the faint beat of a plane's engine. But he could not be sure of this. These days he often heard noises in his head which had nothing to do with the outside world. Not long after the plane's noise he thought he heard, so distant that it might have been the strident call of some insect around the stream, the sound of a bugle. That was a familiar noise in his head and it was a sound that wakened

old memories in him of his young days farther south when
he had met the Belgian troops. They had had bugles.

Below him the flamingoes gathered above the misty lake
and rose in their morning flight until the sun caught at
their wings and made them gleam as they beat the air in
short dagger thrusts. And at the head of the flock as
always flew the black flamingo and seeing it N'Dene
nodded approvingly. Then, as they settled back to the
water, he heard below him the sound of his people stirring
in the homestead, the call of women and children, and he
turned away in anger, remembering suddenly his shrewish
daughter, and began to climb the hill towards the spot
where he had found the sick white man.

Around N'Dene's neck as he climbed the can-opener
which Sinclair had given him banged against his bony
chest in company with the magic whistles and other
charms he wore.

*　　　*　　　*

The Auster Aiglet had a range of over five hundred
miles and Amra had seen to it that the fuel tanks were
full, thirty-two imperial gallons. From the Bomu river,
halfway to the lake, Sinclair had turned south. He had
to have good light for the landing, so he had run south for
half an hour and then had turned back. Before the
mountains had begun to rise from the grey, misty half-
light he had seen the great flush of colour spread in the
east as the sun, still hidden, came shouldering its way upwards, forcing the day to life with a careless pyrotechnic
display.

A little later he picked up the great pile of flat rocks that
marked the cave position. He went in low over it and
looked down. There was no sign of life except for a troop of
baboons that galloped away across the mountainside. Then
he put the nose up and climbed, turning away to the south
again to find the little plateau which he had spotted before.

Amra said, "You not going to land at lake, boss?"

Sinclair smiled. "Not yet, Amra. There's something I've got to do first."

"What, land up here on the mountains, boss?"

"That's it, Amra."

"But, boss . . ." Amra's words trailed away.

There was plenty of light now for the sun was above the horizon and the rocks and trees below were casting long, black morning shadows. He went in over the plateau as low as he could, watching the ground below. This was not going to be easy. He had to land safely and in such a way that he could turn and leave the plane ready for a take-off.

He made two runs above the plateau, his eyes watching the ground below. It was flat enough, but here and there a group of boulders rose from the brown, sun-scorched grass, and for all he knew the grass might hide anything. He circled away to the west, the ground photographed in his mind clearly, already his line picked, and then came in from the south again. He kept the nose of the plane headed on the beginning of the line of trees which marked the eastern edge of the plateau. As he lost height Amra's head came up to his shoulder.

Sinclair half turned and winked at him.

"Anything goes wrong, Amra—you jump for it quick."

"Yes, boss. But nothing go wrong. You fly like a bird."

He smiled to himself. He was confident, but not as confident as Amra.

He came in, flattening out, watching the dun coloured, rock-marked ground ahead rushing back at him. Then he put her down gently as though she were a flying egg and the shell must not be hair-cracked. She touched, bumped once, then bumped again and then was rolling, swaying awkwardly for a while. She evened out as he throttled back and he put the rudder over, veering away from a pile of rocks fifty yards ahead. She came to rest docilely ten yards to one side of the rocks.

Beside him Amra grunted and aid, "Man, boss. How you dare do that. That you got to show me."

"One day, Amra. Now—out." He cut the motor and they jumped out.

Between them they manhandled the Auster round so that she was ready for a take-off. When this was done he lit himself a cigarette and gave Amra one. They stood by the side of the plane and the sun was warm on their faces. A pleasant feeling of elation possessed Sinclair. So far, so good, and the worst was over. All he had now was a two-hour trip to the cave and back and his hands would be full of diamonds.

Amra said, "What now, boss?"

"You stay here, Amra, and watch the plane. I'll be gone two, maybe three hours. When I get back . . . Well, we'll fix the rest then."

And he meant that. So far he was deliberately not thinking too far ahead. He would go down to the lake and see Nina. He had no idea what might happen down there. He would have to wait and see. But it was safe enough to go down because he guessed that Major Winton would still be off on his wild goose chase. Nina would either come with him or she wouldn't. One way or the other he would be off and he could drop the plane somewhere and —if the boy agreed—Amra could fly it back to Voyadis. If not, he would find some way of letting Voyadis know where his plane was. It could all be arranged, and then there was the whole of Africa to hide him and the whole of the world beyond Africa, too.

He left Amra, sitting in the shadow of the plane and smoking. He went right-handed across the plateau and reached the fringe of trees which from that point swept downwards in a thick mass to some hidden valley. Keeping in their shade he worked his way forward. A mile ahead was a ridge of rocks that masked the sudden break from plateau to the far slopes that led down to the lake and to the west towards the mountainside that held the cave where Hadlow lay buried.

He had almost reached the ridge of rocks and was still

in the cover of the trees when he heard a sound that made
him halt suddenly. He stood there, listening, not sure
whether he had heard aright. A monkey screamed somewhere deep in the trees and there was a screeching of birds
far away, and then silence. Then into the silence came the
sound he had first heard. There was no mistake this time.
It was a bugle call. Not one call, not one bugle, for the
first call was answered and then two or three bugles called
together.

What the devil could it be, he asked himself? There was
no settlement within a hundred miles of this place. The
lake was a good ten or fifteen miles away. These calls
were less than a mile away. He looked back towards the
Auster. So far as he could make out Amra was still
squatting in the shadow of the plane and apparently had
heard nothing.

The chorus of bugles ceased and then one bugle called
again, briefly, imperiously. Sinclair turned and worked
his way into the trees. The scrub was thick underneath
them and he had to force his way through. But after a
while the undergrowth thinned out and he was going
downhill rapidly. Then the trees began to thin and he
came out on to the edge of a wide sweep of almost parklike
grassland studded with trees and falling gently away to a
long valley. Sinclair stood in the cover of the last line of
trees and stared with amazement.

The valley curved sinuously away to the north, ending
in a narrow, gorge-like defile through which the river ran.

The river for most of its course hugged the far side of
this valley, snaking along the foot of a tall stretch of
mountain cliff that rose abruptly in grey jagged pinnacles
and buttresses. On this side of the river the valley bottom
was level grass land, marked here and there by clumps of
trees and shrubs and then sloping gradually upwards towards the massed trees at whose edge he stood.

Three hundred yards below him was a collection of
grass-thatched huts. They were laid out in neat lines to

form three sides of a great square and the river side of the square was completed by a palisade of bamboos and timber.

Sinclair stood there, wondering if he were dreaming. The whole thing had an Alice in Wonderland touch, but a touch that was grimmer and more threatening than the macabre inconsequences of any fairy tale. Even before he had taken it all in, he was already understanding everything, his mind leaping ahead and his memory racing backwards, weaving a pattern that swiftly made sharp vivid sense to him.

Over the bare ground of the great square formations of men were drawn up. At least two hundred of them, he estimated. They were all Africans and they were all dressed the same, in greenish coloured battle-dress with American army type steel helmets, and they all carried short-barrelled carbines. By the huts which were nearest to him he saw three Bren carriers with their crews at their sides, and away on a knoll to the right of the bamboo palisade he could see a group of men around a field gun which he thought might be a twenty-five pounder. He could see no more field guns, but looking round he spotted at various points across the valley floor small machine gun posts, all of them manned. But the most curious thing was some preparation which was going on down by the river. Along about a half a mile of its length men were busy pouring something from large cans into the water.

A bugle shrilled below him, and he saw now the flash of the sun on the instrument. The bugler was standing at the foot of a flagpole that marked the centre of the square. At the masthead of the pole, streaming away in the steady morning breeze was a large green flag and in its centre was some black device which after a few moments Sinclair made out to be a flamingo in full flight.

As the bugle call died away, he saw the Azandes from the river form into small platoons and begin to run back towards the encampment. At the same time the square below him broke into a frenzy of orderly movement, men breaking rank, wheeling away in small companies and platoons, everyone going at full pace, ant-like and orderly. The field gun suddenly opened fire with a sharp bark and there was the long whistle of a shell. Far away over the river on the steep rock face the shell exploded and a plume of dust rose lazily into the sunlit air. And now began, as though specially laid on for him, a demonstration which was so unexpected that he stood amazed. If he had been a visiting general it could not have been better done. Watching it, there was no doubt in his mind that only a man of considerable military training could have taken these raw Azandes and instilled them with such discipline and precision—and that man he was sure must be Winton.

The one field gun went on pounding away at different points on the cliff face and the Azande army spread out in a great fan advanced on the river with the Bren gun carriers covering their flanks. The machine guns chattered away on fixed lines of fire, pouring a stream of bullets over the men's heads and cutting great swathes of pluming dust in the ground ahead of them.

When the men were twenty yards from the river, the long stretch of water burst into a wavering, roaring barrier of flames as the petrol which had been poured into it was ignited at various points. Bugles clamoured shrilly from the centre and flanks and, with bullets pouring over their heads, the men leapt into the water and fought their way across through the flames. Sinclair watched them coming out on the other side, beating at their clothing to extinguish the flames, and then, firing their carbines from the hips, they launched an attack on the cliff while the field gun pounded away at the rocks above them. They went up commando fashion, some roping themselves and others scrambling up by hand holds alone; and all the time the valley echoed and re-echoed to the sound of firing. In a few moments the whole cliff face was swarming and black with the figures of the men. The field gun ceased fire.

A bugle blew one long imperious note and all other

firing ceased. Sinclair watched the men come down the cliff face and re-form into companies at the foot. They came back towards the camp at a fast trot, swarming through the river where the flames had now died away. As they came back they chanted some song whose sound came up to him husky, defiant and barbaric. In three-quarters of an hour the whole thing was over and the companies reforming in the great square.

The Bren carriers came roaring across the dusty sur-face, long trails of dust reaching behind them, and pulled up by the flagstaff. From the leading carrier a man jumped down and turned to face the assembled men. He raised an arm in salute and began to address them. Sinclair could not hear the words. He watched this one lone figure standing before the men, his arm working and every now and then a roar of approval coming up from the massed men. The lone man held all his attention. His face was grimed with dust and sweat and his green battle-dress was black now with water from the river crossing. Even at this distance Sinclair could see the tall, strong body alive with pride and power and exultation. The man was Mabenge.

He had known it from the moment the man had leapt from the Bren carrier. In a way, he had known it from the moment he had come out of the fringe of the trees and seen the camp, known that this must be the man who had brought about this assembly in the heart of Africa. No-body had to tell him what it all meant. The Congo just now was a great tree, laden with ripe, hanging plums, waiting to be gathered. And what better place to assemble and train the spoilers of the tree than this valley, hidden away in the heart of the Azande country.

Suddenly aware of his own position, knowing that there was danger now for him if anyone should realise that he had seen this, he turned away back into the trees, a host of questions alive in his mind.

The slope steepened and his feet slipped on the dead

leaves as he climbed. He reached to grasp a branch to help himself up a sharp bank and, as he did so, a man stepped out from behind a tree at the head of the bank. Sinclair halted, one hand still holding the branch, the whole of his weight hanging backwards.

It was an Azande, steel-helmeted, clad in battledress, his hands cradling a carbine that pointed directly at Sinclair. Sinclair remained where he was and he saw, crudely sewn to the breast of the battledress, a black patch of cloth in the shape of a flying flamingo. The man came two steps forward and said something in a language which Sinclair did not understand. But the meaning was obvious in the quick tip of the carbine muzzle towards the valley below.

Sinclair pulled himself forward, throwing himself at the man's feet. He lunged with his shoulder at the man's legs. The Azande tried to jump backwards, but he was too late. Sinclair's shoulder took him on the legs and he fell backwards. As he went he swung the carbine downwards jabbing at the body below him and firing it at the same time. The searing heat of the explosion beat over the top of Sinclair's head and the bullet thudded into the ground behind him.

Sinclair threw himself on the man, felt him twist away, caught him by an arm and flung his weight across him. For Sinclair, seeking to get a hold on the Azande's throat, it was as though he held beneath him a part of the earth that sought to rise up and unseat and overwhelm him. He felt the warm skin of the man under his hands, got a grip on his throat and began to squeeze. Under him the long body leapt and convulsed in a sudden frenzy of panic as breath was denied it. They rolled together and the bank which Sinclair had climbed was beneath them unexpectedly. They went over the eight foot drop together in a crashing of branches and a hissing of dead leaves and twigs. The Azande's face was dark and distorted, close to Sinclair's, and then as they pitched together down the bank and into the trees at the bottom Sinclair's head was crashed against a tree trunk He went out and down, deep down into a warm blackness.

\*　　\*　　\*

When he came to he was lying on a camp bed in a grass-thatched hut. Through the open doorway he could see the back of an Azande guard and beyond him the dusty, drill-beaten ground of the square. A party of Azandes was practising bayonet drill on the far side with a straw stuffed dummy that swung from a gibbet.

Sinclair rolled off the bed and sat for a moment holding his head in his hands. His forehead was throbbing from the blow it had taken against the tree trunk. He groped in his pocket for a cigarette and lit one. As he drew at the cigarette he was telling himself that he had landed himself right in the soup. He should have guessed that the valley would be guarded. Mabenge would not want strangers, white or black, wandering about the place.

Against the far wall of the hut was a table and on it stood a tin wash bowl full of water and a towel and a cake of soap beside it. Sinclair got to his feet and went to the table. He washed his face and hands and felt better. The guard turned and watched him through the open doorway, his face expressionless.

Sinclair said, "I want to see Mabenge."

He did not know whether the man had understood. But the guard turned away and he heard him call to the left across the square. Sinclair looked at his watch. It was almost eleven o'clock. Amra would still be waiting up by the plane and by now would be beginning to wonder what had happened to him. Another Azande appeared outside and came in, carrying a couple of cans of beer, an opener for them and a rough tumbler made from the bottom of a whiskey bottle. He put them down on the table and went out without a word.

Sinclair opened a can of beer and drank. It was cold and delicious.

It was midday before Mabenge appeared. He walked in, wearing green battledress, his feet bare, and sat on the end of the bed while Sinclair cocked himself on the edge of the rough table.

"I'm sorry about your accident," Mabenge said pleasantly, "but the guard was only doing his duty."

"I almost had my head blown off by his carbine."

Mabenge rubbed a hand over his chin and ignored the remark.

"What are you doing out here anyway, Mr. Hadlow?"

"The name is Sinclair. You know I'm not Hadlow."

"Yes, I know. But what were you doing out here?"

"Having a look round. I like to get to know the countryside."

Mabenge smiled. "You have got to know quite a lot, haven't you?"

"It seems I have. Just what goes on up here?"

"You have seen. Major Winton and I are training an Azande army. Men from my nation have been coming up here in batches for the last six months. They get a month's training and then go back to their villages to wait."

"For what?"

"For the moment when we move. Do I have to explain more than that? You know the confused state of the Congo. It is time the right people stepped in and began to restore order."

"And you and Major Winton are the right people?"

"We believe so. With the Azande nation as a nucleus we are going to build a new empire in the Congo . . . and, who knows, perhaps ultimately a new Africa. Great things begin small."

"And what kind of empire is it going to be?"

Mabenge rubbed the heel of his bare right foot in the dust of the floor. "What do you expect me to say? A

democratic empire? A communist one? That's what you
would expect, isn't it, from a man like me, some dream
built on an ideology."

"Frankly, yes."

"Well, you would be wrong. This is going to be an
empire. Just that. It will be hard and ruthless when it has
to be. In the beginning men's lives won't count because to
conquer and rule men have to die. Both the major and I
are ambitious men. First of all we have to come to power.
There will be no scruples about the way we do it. A handful of democratic or communist scruples in the beginning
can wreck everything. We are going to conquer, to
possess, to rule . . . just that."

It was said without heat but with a quiet determination
that carried a surprising force.

"Anyone who gets in the way, goes under?"

Mabenge nodded. "Join us or perish. One purpose.
You have seen the mistakes my other countrymen have
made and are still making. Lumumba, for instance,
blowing with every wind and finally being murdered.
And Tshombe . . . a mountebank. None of them has any
real purpose. They expect some miracle. Maybe they
even pray for some miracle. The major and I need no
prayers. We have men and arms."

Sinclair was silent for a moment. This man spoke too
earnestly, with too much dedication, to let even the edge of
melodrama mark his words. He spoke, too, as an educated
man, fully aware of the political theories which he was
determined should not bedevil his own enterprise. He
had a point there, too, thought Sinclair. You couldn't
make omelettes without breaking eggs. Heads would be
broken, lives would be lost. Behind the educated man
was the Azande to whom a life meant nothing. Purpose
in him was supported by the primitive hardness of tribal
life.

"And which of you," asked Sinclair, "is to be Emperor
when the time comes?"

Mabenge's long, generous mouth tightened a little. Then he smiled.

"You think two men, two brothers, for we are that, will quarrel over the kill? One seek to destroy the other in the moment of triumph? No . . . the major and I have a perfect understanding. I shall be Emperor, King, Altissimo, whatever we decide to call it, because my people can make that demand. I make it also. We are a proud nation. Once we were great. We shall be great again. My own blood is the blood still of our past kings. It is not only European countries that have had a belief in the divine right of kings, a belief in the sanctity of the royal blood."

"And the major? What does he become—Secretary of State for War?"

Mabenge gave a little laugh. "He becomes what he wishes. You do not understand the major. He is a small man physically. All his life he has resented this. He is an efficient, intolerant man who has lived in this country away from his fellows largely because their lack of his hard qualities has sickened him. I do not know exactly what he wants other than money and power. This country will be rich and when it is ours we shall also be rich and powerful. I think, quite simply, that is what he wants. He wants his name known in history, he wants wealth, he wants to command—there will be room for us both."

"I think you are both crazy."

"That could have been said of Napoleon and so many others—in the beginning."

"And look how they finished, all those others."

"What does that matter? They are dead but their names live and while they lived they lived fully. You know . . ." Mabenge paused, looking at him intently, "it is interesting talking to you about this. It becomes clear that you are quite unlike either of us. You have no ambition. Also, not once have you asked me what your position is."

"It seems quite clear to me. I've stumbled on your secret. Either I give you my word that I'll say nothing about it and you let me go—or you don't take my word and you keep me here until such time as you begin your move, and I have nothing to tell, since it will be already known."

"And would you give your word?"

"If I did would you believe me?"

"No."

"Then the point doesn't arise." Sinclair lit a cigarette and began to open the remaining can of beer. As he poured it into the rough glass, he said, "How do you keep your beer so cool?"

"The major and I have a small refrigerator which is worked from butane gas. It is a little luxury he allows himself up here. Ice for his drinks and cold beer."

"Where is the major now?"

"I've sent a runner for him. He has been out two days looking for the grave of Hadlow. But, Mr. Sinclair, to return to your position. I have to keep you here because I cannot trust you. But I have another proposition to make."

"What?"

"You fly a plane. Why not join us? One day we shall have planes, many of them."

"No dice, Mabenge. I don't have that kind of ambition. Tell me—does Nina Winton know all about this scheme?"

Mabenge rose slowly.

"She does."

"And she approves."

"No."

"Yet you trust her to keep your secret?"

"It is not quite the same thing as with you, Mr. Sinclair. With you I have been very frank. With Miss Winton, the major has somewhat understated our intention. It is a democratic movement which will restore order in the Congo. Women are not political creatures, Mr.

Sinclair. She is concerned with his safety more than any-thing else. Although they don't get on very well, she has a great loyalty towards him and would do nothing to wreck his plans."

"You mean the wool has been pulled over her eyes."

"It is another way of expressing it. Yes ˮ

"So?"

Mabenge shrugged his shoulders. "With luck the major will be back sometime tomorrow. We can thrash the whole thing out then. And until then I suggest that you think over what I have said. We could use you. And you would be well paid."

"To drop home-made bombs on villages down the line to Leopoldville and places west? No thanks. I've had one dose of that."

"Nevertheless, think about it." He was almost at the door, but he halted and then, with a surprising note of naïveté said, "What did you think of our demonstration?"

"First-class."

"Thank you. By the way, we found your plane and I have put a guard on it."

When he was gone Sinclair sat down on the side of the bed and finished the last of the beer. He was not worrying about Amra. Mabenge had not mentioned him, so he must have made off. He could well look after himself. He could make his way to the lake and get a lift back on the next store plane.

That Mabenge had been so frank and open about his plans did not surprise him. There was a vanity in the man which was stronger than any caution. He had met it in other educated Africans, this almost childish delight in revealing their cleverness. Not that he didn't have some-thing to be pleased about—assembling and training these men had taken a lot of organisation. The future was wide open to them. They were going to tear this country apart and then put it together again in the way that suited them. No fancy tie-ups with democracies or any other ocracies.

There was a big idea behind the whole thing, of course. A great Azande nation again. A black Roman Empire. But Mabenge and Winton were not going to be gentlemanly about the way they did it. There was no doubt in his mind, for instance, that if the circumstances had warranted it on his capture, Mabenge would have stood him out in the square before a firing squad and filled him with lead and have thought nothing of it. Winton as well, obviously. And that was going to happen to a lot of people when they got started.

He had never been greatly interested in politics. There was a natural distrust in him of all politics and politicians. This thing stuck in his throat mostly because of the ruthless frankness behind it. Mabenge would bomb and shell villages and towns and when it was over build himself a palace on the banks of the Congo, worthy of an Azande prince, from which to rule an empire.

# CHAPTER TWELVE

Amra had spent the night crouched on the lower branch
of a tree on the valley side. He had slept very little,
not only because of the discomfort of his branch, but because he was still amazed at the things which had happened and which he had seen.

The previous morning when Sinclair had not returned
after three hours, he had left the shadow of the Auster
and gone over to the trees, following the route which
Sinclair had taken. Except that he had had instructions
from Sinclair to stay by the plane he would have gone
long before to investigate the sound of firing and bugle
calls which had come from beyond the trees.

The moment he had entered the trees he had heard the
sound of men moving up the valley side and had just had
time to take cover before three armed Azandes in battledress had passed him. He had followed them and seen
them find the plane. One man had remained on guard
and the other two had gone back down into the valley,
followed at a safe distance by Amra. The settlement in
the valley had been a great surprise to him, and he had
climbed the tree he now occupied and watched, convinced that Sinclair was somewhere in the camp, and
equally convinced that he was in trouble. Until daylight
had gone he had watched, and he had seen Mabenge go
once into a hut facing the square and then, after a time,
come out. Food had been taken to the hut twice before
darkness came. Amra had guessed that Sinclair was in the
hut. At night he went down under cover of darkness to
try and get near. But there had been a guard at the back
and another in the front and Amra had withdrawn to his
tree.

He crouched there now as the sun rose and he looked longingly towards the river, for he was very thirsty. Food he did not care about much, but water he knew he would have to have soon. He decided that he could work through the trees northwards along the valley flank and then, a couple of miles from the camp, come down and using the tall grass cover reach the river and drink.

He was about to climb down from his tree when he heard a breaking of branches and the sound of men coming down the hill behind him. He knew that this could not be the guard at the plane being changed for he had already seen the reliefs the day before, and heard them late at night, going up the valley side some way to his right.

He climbed higher into the foliage of the trees. A few moments later the men passed beneath him. There were two Azandes, naked except for their *rokas*, and with them Major Winton. They went down the valley side and into the camp and Amra saw Major Winton go into a large grass-thatched hut to one side of the square. Although the longing for water was fierce in him, Amra decided to stay where he was a little while longer. This whole thing was very puzzling and somewhere in the heart of the puzzle he was sure that there was trouble for his boss. And if his boss was in trouble there had to be something he could do about it.

A bugle blew thinly higher up the valley. Then another answered it from the square and he saw a small party of men march to the flagstaff and form up. The bugle blared again, long and like some strange bird call, throating joyfully into the new morning, and as the call echoed about the valley Amra saw the green flag suddenly break from the masthead. It hung limply for a moment and then the breeze took it, licking its folds free and he saw the black emblem of the flying flamingo.

*       *       *

Sinclair was awake as the morning bugles went.

Through the open doorway of the hut he saw the green flag float free over the square and watched the quick military snap and precision of the little party of Azande soldiers as they presented arms to it. He smiled to himself as he thought of Winton . . . discipline would be drilled into these men in their month's training . . . discipline, and every order carried out without a question. He remembered the way the men had crossed the river of fire. God help anyone who got in their way when they started to move.

A few moments later an Azande came into the hut carrying his breakfast. It was a tin mug full of goat's milk and a slab of millet cake with a piece of cold fish on top of it. It looked thoroughly unappetising but to his own surprise he ate and drank with gusto and found the fish extraordinarily good.

Ten minutes later he was being marched between two guards out of the hut and along the top side of the square to another, much bigger hut in the far corner. A long, sloping canvas awning had been stretched along the face of this hut and as he approached he saw that Mabenge and Winton were sitting under it. Both of them rose as he was brought into the shade and Mabenge gave an order to the two guards. The men fell back about a dozen paces and, motionless under the sun, stood on guard with their carbines cradled on their hips. Winton without a word motioned Sinclair to take a spare camp chair that stood between his and Mabenge's. As Sinclair sat down he caught the smell of coffee coming from the hut behind them and had an immediate longing for it. Coffee for the high command, goat's milk for prisoners. Maybe, he told himself, he ought to take the job with them and get in on the good things of life.

Winton stared at him pugnaciously, wrinkling his thick brows and screwing up his mouth. For a moment he looked like some ape puzzled by the antics of a strange animal, undecided whether to smash it with a blow or to let his amusement at its capers run. Then, unexpectedly, he smiled.

"Would you like some coffee, Sinclair?"

"Thank you."

Mabenge called into the hut and in a few moments an orderly came out with a tray and poured coffee for them. In the meantime, Winton went on, "Mabenge has explained all this to you?" He waved his hand towards the square and the squads of men who were forming up to begin their day's exercises.

"The black empire—yes."

"You don't approve?"

"Frankly, no."

"You hold strong political views, perhaps?"

"No. But there's a properly constituted government in the Congo trying to work things out. The United Nations are there. They all want a chance to work things out."

"Muddlers!" snapped Winton.

"That's normal, isn't it? All new governments have to muddle through until they find themselves. But anyway, you asked me a question and I've answered it."

Winton nodded and sipped at his coffee. "It's unimportant, anyway, what you think. So far as you are concerned the real issue is something quite different. Are you surprised that I haven't been able to find the place where you buried Hadlow?"

"Not very. I only had the vaguest idea myself." Sinclair drank some of his coffee and lit himself a cigarette. He had a quick premonition of what was coming, an unpleasant glimpse of trouble ahead. Casually, he went on, "But if he can't be found that's too bad. Meanwhile, I'm here, and I know about your army. What next—I'm to be a prisoner here until you start moving?"

Winton scratched at his chin and the rasp of the stubble was crisp sounding. "Let us stick to the point—which is Hadlow." He glanced at Mabenge. "Tell him."

BLACK FLAMINGO

"Behind us in this hut," said Mabenge, "we have a two-way transmitter. In Bisaka Voyadis has one. We don't communicate very often. You must have wondered, Mr. Sinclair, where all the arms and equipment we need come from?"

"I see. Voyadis gets them for you. Who flies them in?"

"They come in direct from just over the Sudan border. Voyadis arranges for it—and we have to pay for them of course. The payment is the hardest part of the business so far. And there is much more we need before we can move."

"Don't get side-tracked. Tell him," said Winton impatiently.

Mabenge said, "I spoke to Voyadis early this morning. You caused a great deal of excitement in Bisaka by your break out, Mr. Sinclair. You steal a plane and you fly out here. You might have been expected to land at the lake, perhaps to see Miss Winton. But you didn't. Why did you land where you did?"

"Because I left Bisaka in a rush. I wanted to squat down somewhere for an hour or two and think out where I should go, look at my maps. You can't do that in the air."

"Not because you wanted to pay a visit to Hadlow's grave?"

"Why on earth should I want to do that?"

"You know why," said Winton. "Don't beat about the bush. Damn it, Voyadis tells us that you were arrested for using false papers, but that was only an excuse to hold you. There's a man in Bisaka from the Diamond Corporation who was really responsible for your arrest. Don't fool around, Sinclair. You know that Hadlow had diamonds on him . . ."

Sinclair looked from one to the other. Winton slumped a little in his chair, one leg crossed on the other, the nails in his bush boots shining, a tense, coiled-up figure holding down his energy and impatience uneasily; and then Mabenge, calm, all his strength easily marshalled, handling his power ably and ready to use it without a shred of compassion. He had nothing to hope for from them, and no advantage to be gained by pretending not to understand them.

"Yes, I know now."

"Those diamonds belong to us." Winton's head shot forward turtle-like on his scraggy neck.

"I was told that they belonged to the Kasai mines. That they were stolen."

"So they were. Mabenge has a brother, educated like himself, who works down there. He arranged it. But once stolen the diamonds belong to us."

Sinclair smiled and shook his head. "It's a nice moral point. I'll grant it to you, with this reservation—once they are stolen, they belong to anyone who can get his hands on them. That's why I was going to have a crack at them. But if you can't find the grave, then I'm going to have just as much trouble. Hadlow's under a beobab tree somewhere over there . . ." His hand waved to the mountains behind them.

Mabenge said, "Your imagination is not really working at all yet, Mr. Sinclair. The facts are these. You know exactly where the grave is?"

"No, I don't."

"I didn't expect you to say yes. But you do know. You broke out of jail and you landed somewhere near the grave in order to get the diamonds. The next fact is—and this is where you haven't used your imagination—you are going to tell us exactly where it is."

"Am I?"

"You haven't a hope, Sinclair. Be sensible," put in Winton. "We need every penny we can get for the equipment and arms we still lack. There's been too much damned delay in this already. We've got to get moving quickly. It's up to you. You can tell us and then sit here in reasonable comfort until we're ready to let you go. Or, you can insist on doing it the hard way."

Sinclair said nothing. Although these two men had been talking to him with a show of reasonableness which, to anyone watching, would have given the impression of an amiable discussion with no great issue involved, he had slowly been becoming aware of a disturbing reality. Both of them were fanatics. Not raving. But quietly and inflexibly fanatical to the point where they would take any risk and be untouched by any human feeling if it meant a check to their plans. Here they were in the centre of Africa, a black man and a white man, both dreaming of an empire, a pair of future tyrants, dictators, El Supremos or whatever name they would eventually decide to take, and they were as mad as hatters. Their madness was the kind that brought trouble and tragedy to other people. They had built this army so far on a shoe-string. God knew where the original money had been scraped from . . . maybe they were already selling concessions in the future state to others as fanatical as themselves. But they needed more . . . sixty thousand pounds' worth of stuff to set the avalanche rolling and only he stood in their way. It was a hell of a position and his good sense told him to jump clear at once. He'd never seen himself in the role of a world saver. All he wanted was to wander along in his own disorganised way, taking what came of the things he liked and dodging the things which promised trouble. And here, if ever, was something to be dodged.

He said calmly, "And what do you call the hard way?"

Mabenge stood up and came behind Sinclair's chair.

"Look across to the far side of the parade ground, Mr. Sinclair. To the right of the bayonet practice dummy."

Sinclair looked out at the sun-swept, dusty stretch of ground. Not far away an instructor was taking a Bren gun to pieces before a group of Azandes. A file of men came loping by, their bare feet smacking at the hard earth, their carbines carried at the trail, and disappeared through an

opening in the palisade. Voices barked instructions and
the air was veiled with a faint ochre haze of rising dust.
To the right of the bayonet dummy, swinging idly now,
straw leaking from its body, a man was spread out on the
ground. He was naked except for a loin cloth. He lay on
the ground, the sweat shining on his black skin, and his
arms and legs had been pegged out wide in the shape of an
untidy X. His head rolled occasionally from side to side,
and with each movement a cloud of flies rose from it and,
as Sinclair watched, he saw the great black body arch suddenly against the restraining cords on wrists and ankles.

"Yesterday," said Mabenge, "that man stole a knife
from one of his fellows. To every man who comes up here
certain things are explained . . . discipline, comradeship
and a sense of destiny. These are Azande, my people, and
they are soldiers. All day he will be pegged out there and
his lesson will be learnt."

"For stealing a knife? And you have swiped sixty
thousand pounds' worth of diamonds? A bit mixed up,
isn't it?" But though he spoke lightly, Sinclair's eyes
were still on the man.

At his side Winton said, "The choice is yours, Sinclair."

The choice was all his. He knew that well enough, and
if anyone had put the situation to him hypothetically in
the past he knew that he would have answered without
hesitation that a man would be a bloody fool to take such
punishment for diamonds, for anything.

Behind him Mabenge said, "You might stand a day of
it, Mr. Sinclair. I should say you would. But then comes
the night when you get some respite, but all the time you
know the next day is coming. . . . You'd never last beyond
a few hours of the next day. You'd be frantic to talk. So,
why not do it now? Just tell us where Hadlow is buried."

Sinclair stood up and turned, facing them both. He
knew he was a fool and even as he prepared to speak he
kept calling himself a fool, telling himself to be sensible,
but there was something inside him beyond analysis which

was like a great cold anger that paralysed any movement or words which threatened to betray it. He had to follow that coldness, against his will, against all reason, because it was something new in him and could not be ignored.

He said evenly, "Thank you for the coffee."

He turned away from them, and began to walk out into the sunlight. They let him go, four, five, six paces, before they did anything. Then Winton barked an order at the two guards who were watching the approaching Sinclair. Immediately the two men came forward and took him by the arms. He made no effort to resist them. Effort and resistance now, he acknowledged, lay under the direction of the coldness in him and at the moment it prompted him to no action.

\*       \*       \*

Amra, from his tree, saw them take him to the far side of the square. He was stripped to the waist. There were six men with him, and also Mabenge who stood aside, watching the operation. He was stretched out on the ground and the quick thuds of the mallets as the men knocked the wrist and ankle pegs into the ground came sharply up to Amra.

He watched, not puzzled now, but full of anger at the thing which was being done to his boss, and knowing that he must do something about it. What had his boss done that they were pegging him out like this? Major Winton he knew was in the camp. Was it because the major was angry with his boss because he liked Miss Nina? If that were so then the sooner he told Miss Nina the better. She would stop all this. He looked northward up the valley. From flying he had a good eye for ground and he guessed that somewhere over the gorge that closed the valley would be the lake. It would be a good ten miles away.

Amra did not wait to see more. He dropped down from his tree and worked his way back up the slope. From higher up the valley side he could work along in the cover of the massed trees towards the northern end of the valley. He would have to wait now until he came to the gorge through which the river flowed before he could drink. But that was nothing. He had to get to Miss Nina as quickly as possible. To peg out a white man. . . . How could that be done by someone like Major Winton? That Mabenge should do this to one of his own tribesmen was reasonable if the man had offended him. But white men did not do this to one another.

Clear of the camp now, he began to run. Under the trees it was hot and stifling. Soon his body was wet with sweat, but he kept on, going at a steady lope.

\* \* \*

Stripped of his shirt Sinclair was pegged out in the compound only a few yards from the Azande. While they were fixing the thongs of his ankles and wrists to the pegs, he saw the Azande's head turn, the flies swarm up from him. and for a moment the man stared at him dully. Then his eyes closed and, his head relaxing, the flies swarmed back.

For good measure one of the guards tightened Sinclair's trouser belt a couple of notches so that it cut into his waist every time that he breathed. Mabenge watched all this unmoved. But when the operation was complete he came and stood over Sinclair.

"By this evening you will want to talk. Be sensible, Mr. Sinclair, and talk now."

"Go to hell," said Sinclair.

He was left alone, staring up into the cloudless sky where the sun climbed slowly towards its zenith. A few yards away the Azande began to moan gently to himself. Voices came from the huts and the training parties on the parade ground. Now and again a squad of men pounded by him and the air was thick with dust that he drew into his mouth, feeling it harsh and sour tasting in his throat.

He breathed easily at first to ease the bite of the belt about his waist. After a while, under the lash of the sun,

he felt the sweat breaking out all over his body and the
first flies begin to settle on his face and neck.  He shut his
eyes and mouth and breathed slowly through his nose,
trying to ignore the flies.  But every now and then one of
them bit him with a sharp stab of fire that made his body
jerk.

The beat of the sun on his forehead began to feel like a
great brazen hand pressing him down.  Sometime, it could
have been an hour, two hours later, the Azande began to
talk to himself, a long, angry monologue that only ended
when Sinclair, to his surprise, heard himself call out
sharply to the man to shut up.  The Azande was silent.

But a little later when the man began to talk again,
Sinclair let him be.  For some reason, or more truly out of
some impulse which he could not control, he had elected
to put himself to this torture.  He was going to need all the
strength he had.  Some impulse . . . he smiled to himself
grimly at the thought.  The head shrinkers, he supposed,
would say he was doing it for some deep, subconscious
reason, punishing himself, maybe, for something.  Well,
they were welcome to it.  He was here and so far as he was
concerned there was nothing to do but to take each minute
as it came and live no longer ahead than that.

He lay, relaxing himself as much as he could, trying to
ignore the rising consciousness of his body.  The hard
ground bit into his sweat-soaked back, the sun beat against
his face setting up a throbbing in his temples, the tempo
increasing slowly until a drum seemed to be banging away
inside him.  The outside world and his thoughts became
mixed. . . . A bugle blared on the parade ground and he
had a vivid picture of an airfield in Italy, a wind sock stiff
in the breeze, and a squadron lined up for inspection, but
oddly enough when the visiting officers came round on
their inspection he saw that Nina was with them, smart
in khaki drill with blue Air Force tabs, and frowning.  He
winked at her as she passed him but her face was frozen.

Once he was clearly aware of Mabenge standing at his

feet. It was hard to focus steadily on the man because of the sweat and flies that pestered his eyes. He seemed to swim close and then fade away. He noticed that Mabenge held a steel helmet, crooked like a top hat, under his arm, in a respectful way, as though he stood at a graveside. Sinclair shut his eyes and drifted away. . . . He heard the tinkle of ice in a glass and the bar of the hotel was suddenly explosive with laughter. A woman's hand caught at his wrist, her head dipping with a cigarette in her mouth to reach the flame of his lighter. The head came up, wreathed with a quick aura of smoke and it was Nina, smiling at him, her blue eyes alight with laughter. He smiled back, feeling her hand on his wrist still; and he wondered why she had taken up smoking.

The hours passed and the sun dropped slowly. Several times, with a desperation beyond his control, he arched and strained with his body against the bonds that held him to the pegs, and each time that it happened it was some time before he could get hold of himself and force himself to call off the stupid struggle.

# CHAPTER THIRTEEN

THE evening was a long time coming; a lifetime of burning waiting. There were long periods when Sinclair
drifted away entirely from himself, so remote from his body
that there seemed to be no feeling in him. Coming back
from these periods was agony, an agony of being sharply
alive to every sensation in his body. And every time he
came back he found himself arguing bitterly against his
own stupidity. There was no point in enduring this futile
beastliness. In the end—as Mabenge had said—he would
talk. Why not do it now? What he was doing wasn't
logical. He was just punishing himself unnecessarily.
Why prolong it? Nobody was going to hand him out a
medal for doing this. So talk. The diamonds would be
lost to him, but what the hell did that matter? He'd been
content enough before when he had known nothing about
them. He could shrug off their loss without any worry.
What the hell did it matter to him if Mabenge and Winton
got their little army moving; what did it matter if they
went down through the Orientale province, over-ran the
whole of the Congo eventually and made their wildest
dreams come true? It was no affair of his. Why hang on?
All he had to do was to shout for Mabenge and tell him
where Hadlow was. Time and again he arrived at the firm
decision to shout for Mabenge. But at the moment of
resolution it was only to find that he could not do it.

As the sun dropped behind the mountains and the
shadow of the parade ground palisade lengthened across
the dusty earth, a party of men came down and released
the Azande. Twisting his head to one side Sinclair
watched them listlessly. They cut the man's bonds and
jerked him to his feet. One of them threw a bucket of

water over him, and another handed him a pannikin of water to drink. The Azande took the tin in his hands to drink but he had no command over his fingers. The pannikin fell to the ground and the fringe of the spray of spilled water just touched Sinclair's face. It was so cold that it was like the lash of a whip on his sunburnt skin. The pannikin was filled again and this time the Azande held it and drank slowly, his head lowered, his back streaked with dust, the skin crinkled and bitten with marks from the hard ground. Slowly his head came up from the tin and he looked around and down at Sinclair. Momentarily there was a flash of sympathy in his eyes. He jerked the pannikin away from him with a movement of disgust and Sinclair knew that he was ashamed to have drunk his fill before him. The Azande braced his shoulders and turned away, spreading out his hands to hold off the assistance his companions were ready to offer. For Sinclair the sight of that moment of independence was like a great balm.

Time meant nothing after that. It was dusk and then it was dark, and the coolness of the night began to ease his body and he could feel it battered and stiff, coming back under his control. And the flies had gone, which was the greatest relief. He lay there, calmer now and able to think without confusion. And his thoughts were chiefly memories of flying. He saw himself coming in over the hot, yellow fields of Foggia with the studding of grey olive trees below and the women working in the maize patches turning their faces up to him. His memory was crystal clear and penetrating, bringing up faces and places which he had not had in mind for years and years. He remembered flying over Florence with the Arno dried to a brown, frayed piece of string below him, the smashed masonry of the Santa Trinita bridge sprawled across it. He seemed to race through the years in his memory and then suddenly the picture was full of bright, golden morning and a vast cloud of flamingoes going up into the air . . . and he was

bathing with Nina, feeling the smoothness of her brown
shoulders under his hands, seeing the fine web of her fair
hair spread on the water, and her face was so close to him
that he cupped it in his hands and put his lips to hers, en-
joying the water coldness of their contact. And then, in his
ears, he heard her whisper just the one word, "Bill . . ."

It was astonishing how vivid the one word was.

"Bill . . ."

It came again. And this time he knew that it was not in
his memory that he heard it. It was close to him, to his
right, and he came back to the present with a sense of
shock.

In the sky there was the faint looming suggestion of
coming moonlight. The parade ground was a great pool
of inky blackness.

He heard his name again and this time with it the sound
of movement along the ground close to him. A hand came
out and held his wrist. He made an effort to turn, his body
twisting, but the hand shook at his wrist.

"Lie still, Bill. Lie still . . ."

He heard her move again, and then felt the pressure of a
knife working on his right hand bonds. He lay there as
Nina worked her way round him, flattening herself to the
ground all the time, cutting away his other thongs. Then
suddenly her face was close to him and he heard her
swear with a furious, clamped-down anger. Her hand
went under his head and raised it a little, just enough for
her to put the mouth of a water bottle to his lips.

"Not too much . . ."

The bottle was taken away from his lips, but he could
smile to himself because he had tasted that the water was
cut with whiskey.

The bottle was put to his lips again and as he drank she
was talking to him, whispering, telling him what he had to
do. The liquid ran through him like a great frost, making his body tremble. The bottle went from him again
and he lay back, closing his eyes for a moment in a great

luxury of release. He felt her lips on his cheek and he moved an arm and held her to his side, feeling the warmth of her body through her shirt, just holding her and wanting the moment to go on and on. Then, his mind beginning to work, he was sharply aware of what she had done and of the danger which was all around them. Sensing it in him, Nina moved from him.

"You go first," she whispered. "Roll over to the palisade. Amra is waiting the other side of the gap. There are two guards up at the huts. None here."

He shook his head but she knew what he was going to say before he could begin.

"Go first, you bloody fool. If anything goes wrong they won't touch me. You must get away."

"But you're coming too."

"Of course. But I'll stay here until you're away. Go on, Bill—for God's sake!"

He felt her hands on his shoulders, urging him away. Against his will he moved. Slowly he rolled away through the darkness and after a few minutes was at the palisade edge. Awkwardly he raised himself on all fours and crawled along the bamboo wall until he found the gap in it. As he went through it Amra met him, reaching down and taking him by an arm.

Sinclair stood up, his limbs moving awkwardly, and his head swam for a moment.

"Boss. . . . You all right, boss?"

He put a hand on Amra's shoulder and shook him gently. Amra would have moved then, but Sinclair said softly, "Wait."

Eventually Nina came, rising through the gap and then putting her arms around him. She held him closely, the two of them silent.

Amra shuffled his feet impatiently in the dust. Any moment one of the hut guards might take it into his head to make a tour of the parade ground.

From the palisade gap a track made by the Bren gun

carriers ran away towards the river. Tall grasses and shrubs flanked it on either side. They went down it silently, and Sinclair felt his body beginning to respond with the exercise, but there were moments when it betrayed him, when all his muscles seemed to get screwed up and he would stumble. Within five minutes they were at the river and then moving up it.

Nina said, "We can't go back to the lake. That's the first place they'll check."

"The plane?"

"Yes."

"There's a guard on it."

"We can deal with that. Amra and I have a cache of stuff a little further up."

"Your father will never forgive you for this."

"Step-father. And I don't want anything from him. He let Mabenge do this . . . the bastards!"

"Language," he grinned, feeling his lips cracking.

\*　　　\*　　　\*

A mile up the river under a clump of thorn trees, Nina had made her cache. With Amra she had brought two rifles, food, and a bush shirt belonging to Winton. The shirt was a bit tight for him but he was glad she had thought of it.

They wasted no time because there was no guarantee how long it would be before his escape was discovered. But Sinclair insisted on changing the plan she had worked out. Nina wanted to go up to the plane, deal with the guards at first light and then take off.

"No. There's something else we must do first." He explained to her about Hadlow and the diamonds. "They know now that he's buried not far from the plane. Just to go off and leave them free to hunt around. . . . That's not for me. They could easily spot the cave. We can go up and get the diamonds and still be back at the plane by first light."

Nina did not argue. They went back across the valley from the river and began to climb the hillside. When they met the first of the trees they split up. Amra was given a rifle and told to go up to the plane. He was to keep watch on it from the cover of the trees at dawn and they would join him there on their return from the cave. Amra went off by himself into the trees and Sinclair and Nina worked farther to the right along the slope, taking a line that Sinclair hoped would bring him out at the far end of the plateau with only about a couple of miles to go to the cave.

They moved as silently as they could, not talking. There was a lot he wanted to ask her, a lot he wanted to know and he guessed that she, too, had many things to say, but for the moment there was place only for action.

*     *     *

Many things were now mixed up inside N'Dene's head. His old body, it seemed, could still serve him well. Even when it was punished hard a little food and sleep restored it. But his head was different. The things inside it went their own way, and all he could do was to wait and catch at the thoughts as they came, trying to put them in order. The effort of doing this, however, made him angry. He could not remember now how long he had been wandering about the mountains, and, worse still, sometimes forgot what he was supposed to be doing. Then it would come back to him. He had to find the white man's grave. At the beginning of the night he had slept for a while on a rock ledge, but after a few hours he had awakened, cold, and possessed with a feeling that he had no time to waste in sleep if he were to find the grave. Since then he had been wandering, stumbling over rocks and boulders in the darkness. With the coming of the moon the going had been easier. Only he forgot so often where he was supposed to be going or what he was supposed to be doing.

During his sleep in the early part of the night he had had a dream of a snake, a long python that curled up the thin trunk of a tree and then hung, head down, staring at him. It was a dream wasted on him, for he knew the meaning of all dreams. To dream of a snake was good luck when you were young, for it meant long life and one woke and said, 'My soul is long, I shall live long in truth.' But it was a foolish dream for an old man to dream, and it merely added to his crossness. It would have been better to have dreamt about sweet red potatoes for that would have meant he would soon have meat to eat. The thought of meat made his mouth salivate. Then he thought of his grandson, who would have been here with him had it not been for the bitch who was his daughter. He was a good boy and there was much he had to teach him. He would teach him all about dreams, the good and the bad. But first he would have to learn how to remember dreams. One could wake from a dream and then sleep again and remember the dream the next morning. But if on waking one went and made up the night fire and then slept, then the dream would scatter completely from the mind before morning. The boy would become as great as he, N'Dene, in interpreting dreams.

Towards morning, N'Dene found himself out on a spur of the mountains with a deep hanging valley below him. The tip of the spur was piled high with large flat rocks. He remembered the spot well from the past. As a young man he had hunted along this side of the mountain.

He sat down at the head of a loose run of rock rubble and leant his back against a rock. The moon was strong now and the country lay clear below him, and away to his right he could see the rough slopes that led up to the ridge. Now, resting again, he longed for his grandson, for the boy would have prepared him a pipe and carried for him a gourd of millet beer. The thought of beer and not having any made N'Dene give a little snort of anger.

As the sound died away in the quiet night, he heard the clatter of a rock falling. He looked up the slope and clear in the moonlight he saw two people coming down from the ridge. For some time he watched them without any clear comprehension. They were too far away for him to see them in any detail. He drew back into the shadow of his boulder.

The two came down the slope, picking their way quickly but carefully over the broken ground. When they were two hundred yards away he recognised them. One was Miss Nina from the lake. She was wearing a shirt and trousers and he curled his lips disapprovingly at the sight of the trousers. It was like a woman carrying a spear. Then his disapproval went as he saw the man halt and reach to help the girl down a step in the rocks. His face was sharp in the moonlight and N'Dene recognised him as the white man whom he had nursed. This then was the white man who had buried the man named Hadlow. A great contentment went through N'Dene then, for he knew that the termite oracle was being faithful to him.

Without a doubt this man was coming back to take the diamonds which Mabenge needed, the diamonds which the poison oracle had promised should be Mabenge's.

There was no confusion in N'Dene's mind now. He knew why he was here. He sat very still in the shadow of his rock and watched the two. They went carefully down the steep, broken slope, and they went in the manner of people who knew exactly where they were going. Then, surprisingly, memory sharpened in him by his contentment, N'Dene knew where they were going, and for a moment or two he forgot the two people below him and was back in his young manhood. The memory was as bright as a knife blade. One night, all those many, many years back in time, N'Dene had slept in his father's hut and he had dreamt a dream of a woman of the homestead who was already married and in this dream their navels were joined. Waking from the dream, N'Dene had turned round in his bed so that his feet rested where his head had rested for he knew that that was the way to make the woman he desired begin to dream a dream on her part that she also was with him.  And the next morning he had walked by her and looked at her and she had looked at him, and he had left the village without turning back to see if she had followed.  He had come up here to the hills, to the small cave that rested under the spur of mountain which was topped by the great pile of rocks, and sitting within the cave mouth, he had waited and she had come, and the dream he had dreamt and then made her dream had come true.  He smiled to himself at the memory, not only for the pleasure it recalled, but also because of the cunning and knowledge which had been in him to avoid the anger of her husband who, too late, had followed them to the cave.

The two below him passed out of sight and N'Dene got up and followed them, much higher up and working his way out along the spur.  But to keep them in sight now he had to move out to the edge of the drop that fell some fifty yards to the shallow edge of cliff path that led to the mouth of the cave.

He saw the two come to the mouth of the cave and for a moment it looked to him as though the man were going in alone.  He said something to the woman, but she shook her head, and then the two of them went into the cave.

Elated now with his discovery, anticipating already the pleasure which would be Mabenge's when he, N'Dene, would be the one to tell him about the diamonds, he moved forward so that he could keep the cave mouth under observation.

As he moved on the steep slope, his old feet stumbled and he fell.  He threw out a hand to save himself and found the branch of a dead thorn tree.  He hung on to it for a moment, grumbling angrily to himself, while a stream of small stones slid away from him.  Then the branch snapped and he lurched forward and could not save himself on the steep slope.  He fell and rolled and heard the rising chatter of loose stones and then the larger stones and rocks began to move with him, and the noise of their falling rose into

his ears like the sound of a great and angry wind. He
heard the avalanching boulders fight and smash against
one another and his body was caught up in a great spume
of earth and rubble.

He crashed far down and the ground came up and
received him with a violent embrace. He lay there with a
great darkness cloaking his mind, scouring away memory,
filling him with nothingness while all about him the
world roared and exploded with the fierce movement of
the landslide.

*          *          *

Sinclair was standing well inside the cave when the first
fall of stones began. Nina was nearer the mouth where the
moonlight made a slim triangle of light. He saw the first
whip of rocks and rubble across the open mouth of the
cave and then the whole place was roaring with sound as
though they were in a tunnel and an express train were
thundering down upon them.

He ran forward and, grabbing Nina by the arm, pulled
her roughly farther back into the cave with him. Dust and
rock chips swirled into the cave and the air was suddenly
thick and biting. Unable to move or do anything they
stared at the moonlit frame of the cave mouth. With an
astonishing swiftness the bright, jagged aperture was
rapidly swallowed up, eaten down to a slim line and then
finally blocked as rocks and boulders pounded down outside.

Close against him he could feel Nina's body shake and
wince as the thunder of the fall rose, died and then
crashed into a great roar that threatened never to end,
and then suddenly whispered away into silence.

They stood there in the blackness, holding one another.

Eventually he took his arms from her. He felt in his
pockets for matches and found he had none.

"Matches."

He heard her move and groped out and found her hand

with a box of matches in it. He struck one and momentarily saw her face, her hair whitened with dust. With the light of the match he gathered up from the floor of the cave some hanks of loose grass which had been blown into the place and twisted them together to make a rough torch. He lit it and holding it above him went to the mouth of the cave. He was faced with a wall of rocks and boulders, jammed solid with a binding of rubble and earth. Nina came up close to him and he handed her the torch. Without a word between them, Sinclair began to work on the face of the blockage. He pulled away the loose stones and small rocks, but in a short while the torch went out. He stopped working, realising suddenly that he had been tearing and pulling at the blockage in a blind, disorganised way.

He went back to Nina as she struck a match and behind her he could see the shallow-domed rock pile of Hadlow's grave. He put his arm round her shoulders and motioned her to sit down.

"Have you got any cigarettes?"

Nina pulled a packet from her shirt pocket. He lit one for himself from the dying match. Nina shook her head at his offer of a cigarette.

They sat down in the darkness close together and he held her hand in his.

"We've got to figure this out sensibly. No good rushing at it."

"How did it happen?"

"Plenty of ways. Some animal could have set a slide off. We might have done it ourselves coming down here. The thing is, if I'm going to work on that pile we've got to have light. God knows how thick it will be."

"The box of matches is only half full, Bill."

"Then we must scrabble around on the floor and gather up all the grass and twigs and stuff we can find and make torches. We can light one from another. If there's enough stuff we could start a small fire to light the torches from. There should be something in here because I remember bringing in wood for the fire when I first met Hadlow." He put his arm round her and kissed her quickly on the cheek. "We'll get out. It's only a matter of hard labour." But though he said it cheerfully he had his own reservations. For all he knew the mouth could be blocked solidly for yards and would need a bulldozer or a squad of men.

In the darkness, except for the light from an occasional match, they gathered up all they could from the cave floor. There were enough twigs and pieces of wood to make a small fire. When they had this going, there was sufficient light from it to enable them to move easily about the cave. From the dried grass and longer lengths of twigs they made rough torches, and then Sinclair went to work. He tackled the blockage at one side where the rocks were smaller. It was hard work and very soon he had to strip off his shirt. Whenever he needed it, Nina lit a torch and stood close to him, or by the dim firelight she worked with him herself, taking the rocks from him as he freed them and piling them behind her to one side of the cave. At the end of an hour Sinclair had tunnelled about three feet through the block face, making an opening just big enough to crouch in. But when he was three feet in he came up against the smooth face of an enormous slab of rock, wedged at an angle and weighted at the top, he could see, by another great rock, the lower edge of which clamped down on it to form a thick ceiling. He knew at once that it was hopeless to go on tunnelling at this side. He would have to try somewhere else.

He crawled back out of the hole and squatted on the floor, his head dropping, his shoulders heaving from the exertion of his work.

"No good?" Nina crouched by him.

He shook his head. "Not that side. I'll have to try the other."

When he was rested, he started again. They worked on,

both of them, the fire ebbing behind them and then spurting with a meagre flame as Nina attended it, feeding it sparingly from their small store. There was little talk between them for they were both intent on their labour, dust and sweat streaking their faces, their hands torn and cut with the scraping away of rubble and rock chips. Time lost its meaning. There was only the grey, flame-shadowed mass of blockage ahead of them which had become somehow a personality, opposing itself mightily to their small efforts and by its vastness slowly imposing on them a sense of frustration. And when they rested now they lay back on the hard ground, letting their bodies relax, breathing hungrily and finding it harder and harder to force themselves away from the thought that what they were doing was useless.

# CHAPTER FOURTEEN

N'DENE's right arm was broken. Falling, he had been thrown wide to the skirt of the landslide, spewed outwards, and had come crashing to rest against a small tree far down the valley slope.

When he came to, the sky was grey with the coming dawn and he lay where he was for a long while for it was difficult for him to remember what had happened. Slowly his memory came back. When he tried to move, his body was stiff and unwilling and his legs and arms were cut deep with scratches. The uselessness of his right arm angered him at once, and in his anger there was a warmth which helped to restore him.

He got up and climbed slowly back towards the cave. It was very difficult for him to recognise where it had been for a great bite had been taken out of the spur above it and an enormous mass of rock and rubbish bulged from the hillside where the cave mouth had been.

N'Dene stood watching the pile of rocks and listening. He could hear no sounds. That the two people were still in there he was sure. When the fall had begun they had been there and no one could have dug a way out of the great mass. It would take twenty men working all day, working maybe even longer than that, to uncover the cave mouth.

N'Dene turned away and began to climb back up the mountainside. It was not a long way to the valley where Mabenge trained his men and, although the valley was a secret most of the Azandes shared, no one was allowed to enter it unless he was going there for training. Not even he, N'Dene, had been allowed there, and this in the early days had angered him greatly. But now he had to find Mabenge and tell him about the cave. He would go down into the valley and be welcomed there. When he arrived he hoped that Major Winton would be there. It would be good to stand before Mabenge and the white man and tell his story of the cave. He would watch the white man's face and speak his words triumphantly and everyone would know that he, N'Dene, had more cunning and knowledge than this white man whom Mabenge treated like a brother.

He climbed on, his thoughts wandering from time to time but always returning to the triumph in him. His right arm was throbbing now and he held it to his side with his left hand across his breast to stop the pain. Near the top of the ridge he fainted, dropping slowly to the ground. When he came to he could not remember what had happened, but was angry with himself for going to sleep. He struggled on, lurching and stumbling. He turned a corner of a bluff of rocks and disturbed a leopard that was stretching itself on a rock shelf. The beast turned and its mask split with a nervous snarl. It bounded from him, its body flowing easily across the ground, the first rays of the sun lengthening its shadow.

Some time later he saw ahead of him the rim of trees that marked the valley top, but as he went across the plateau towards them there was the movement of men from the far end of the trees and he stopped, puzzled. The men came out of the trees and he saw them move across the open ground to some large object which flashed grey and white under the strengthening sun. N'Dene went towards them. As he got closer he saw that the object was a flying machine and he recognised it as one he had often seen at the lake.

N'Dene shouted and the faces of the men turned towards him. N'Dene went slowly towards them and he saw them now very clearly. Mabenge was there and with him Major Winton and they both carried rifles. Behind them stood about twenty young Azande also carrying rifles.

N'Dene stopped a few yards from Mabenge and touched his forehead with his left hand in greeting.

Mabenge said, "N'Dene, what do you do on the hills so far from your homestead?"

N'Dene breathed deeply through his nostrils, savouring this moment. The pain in his arm was forgotten. His eyes went from Mabenge to the face of Major Winton and he saw the impatient stir of the man's short, wiry body. Let him hold his impatience for he, N'Dene, would speak.

"O, my prince, great Mabenge, it is true I am an old man. I cannot carry a spear or fight with the young men in an *apalanga* when the moment comes, but I have a wisdom and cunning that flies straighter to the truth than any spear flung by a young warrior. It is I, O Mabenge, who have found the diamonds for you. Into your hands they will come for the oracle has spoken it—"

"For God's sake, Mabenge, tell the old man—"

Mabenge's hand went up, silencing Major Winton's impatience. "Let him speak, major."

"I have seen the white man and the white woman go over the hills to take the diamonds and I have followed them. They have entered the cave below the great pile of rocks where the dead white man is buried. And, when they were in the cave, I called to M'Bori to help me, for how should an old man with no strength in his body protect without help what is his master's? M'Bori has sent a great fall of rocks and trapped the two in the cave."

"What?" There was no restraining Winton this time. He came forward to N'Dene. "Are they hurt?"

"They are in the cave." N'Dene spoke over Winton's shoulder to Mabenge. "It will take many men all day to dig them out, but they will be unhurt. They were deep in the cave when the rocks fell. But Mabenge—"

"We must get down there at once. I know the place he means." Winton turned to Mabenge, ignoring N'Dene, and then barked an order at the waiting Azandes. For a moment or two N'Dene was lost in the sudden movement of men and the voice of Winton giving orders. Before he could say any more, the party was heading away across the plateau. But Mabenge did not move.

He called to Winton, "I will follow." Then he turned to N'Dene and there was a warm smile on his face. "N'Dene," he said, "you must forgive the major his haste. But he, too, works for our greatness as you do, and it is like a fire in his blood. Also the white woman is his step-daughter and although she has wronged him, he still names her as part of his family. You have done well. Now go down to the camp and tell them that I have sent you and that they are to give you all you wish." He turned to the one man, the guard on the plane, who had not gone off with the others, and said, "Go with this wise old man for he is hurt and needs help. There is no need to guard the plane now."

The guard came forward a little, but N'Dene raised his left hand and shook it angrily at the guard.

"Let him stay. I do not go to the camp. Listen, O Mabenge, it is wise that the others go to the rocks to open up the cave. But you and I go elsewhere. Do I not know these hills? Do I not know all these parts? And this cave I know. When I was a young man it was there that I knew a married woman from the homestead who came to me out of our dreams. *Aie* . . . so strong was the dream that she came, following me to the cave, and so sure was she of the dream that she bore in her hand two *badiabe* leaves and a gourd of water that we might wash ourselves afterwards. And there too, much later, her husband followed us and from the cave mouth I saw him and could not go out and hide."

Now Mabenge stirred impatiently for he knew that given rein the old man would go on forever, but N'Dene saw the impatience in him and went on angrily, "Listen, O Mabenge, listen for even yet the diamonds may be lost."

Mabenge bowed his head. "I am listening, O N'Dene."

"Then hear, and then follow me. The white man in the cave I know. Did I not nurse him? Is he not full of cunning? Even as I escaped from the woman's husband so might he escape."

\*　　\*　　\*

It was Nina who forced it on them in the end. They had tried the rock blockage in three places and each time they had come up against great rocks barring any further progress.

Exhausted now, taking a spell, with the fire no more than a pin point of glowing embers, she said, "Bill, we're not going to get out. We're just wearing ourselves away by attacking that stuff."

Sinclair, lying back on the cave floor, smoking, nodded his head. "I haven't wanted to say it, but I agree with you. What a bloody mess." He blew cigarette smoke into the air above him, watched the pale cloud thin and fray out in the gloom of the cave and then put out a hand and took hers. "I got you into this. It would have been better—"

"Don't say that. Nobody gets anybody into anything. It happens."

Sinclair laughed drily. "Know what I was going to do? I was going to pinch the diamonds. Sixty thousand quids' worth. And that wasn't all. I was going to disappear with them and have a good time. God knows doing what. And I was going to ask you to come with me. Would you have done?"

"Would it have made any difference if I'd said no?"

"I didn't see anyone else in the picture."

"You didn't see very much. Didn't it occur to you that what you wanted to do was just plain stealing?"

"I didn't put it so bluntly to myself. Damn it, what have the diamond companies done but that? My heart doesn't bleed for them."

"It's still stealing, you fool. Did you really think I would go along with you on those terms?"

Sinclair was silent. He drew on his cigarette and then said, "You know, I've just noticed something."

"Why don't you answer? You've always been honest with me, and I've been honest with you. If I'd said 'No' wouldn't it have mattered to you? I'd thought that there was something between us that . . ." Her hand gripped suddenly at his arm, and she went on, her voice suddenly backed with a note of despair, "Oh God—what a damned silly conversation in a place like this. Bill, Bill—what are we going to do?"

He sat up, but his eyes were not turned to her. He could still see the faint drift of cigarette smoke above him.

"I'll tell you what we're going to do. If we can't get out by the front door then maybe we can get out by the back door." He blew another puff of smoke. "Look at that smoke. And come to think of it we haven't been worried by the fire smoke or the air getting stuffy. See it—it's drifting backwards into the cave. If the draught is being sucked that way, there could be a way out."

Nina sat up alongside him. "Blow it again."

He blew some more cigarette smoke and it was only the faintest trail of whiteness in the gloom about them, but as they watched it drifted steadily away towards the back of the cave.

Sinclair stood up. "Let's have a look."

"We've got about ten matches left."

"When they're gone we'll have to feel our way."

They went to the back of the cave which narrowed down to a small funnel, about two feet high, close to the ground. In the darkness of the cave it was an opening which might easily have been overlooked. Sinclair took the matches and dropping to the floor began to wriggle through. It was a tight fit but there was just enough room for him to pass. The tunnel ran for about eight feet, then broadened so that he had to raise his arm to feel the roof. He crawled farther and raising his hand again could not feel the rock face above him. He stood up cautiously in the darkness and struck a match. A black shape whipped by him with a sudden whirr of wings and the match was blown out by the quick stir of air. He lit another match and shielded the flame with his cupped hand. This time there was no movement from the bat. The thin light, wavering, then growing stronger, showed him that the tunnel had ended in a small circular chamber about six feet wide. Above him the chamber seemed to be without any roof, losing itself upwards beyond the small flame's compass in darkness. He lit a cigarette with the last of the match and blew out smoke. Another match showed him the smoke being drawn smartly upwards. Hope now began to work in him. This funnel only had to go upwards forty or fifty yards and it must bring them somewhere close to the surface. With luck there might be an exit somewhere on the far side of the gigantic pile of rocks that crowned the spur.

He crawled back through the tunnel to Nina, and told her what he had discovered.

"The funnel looks as though we can climb it. You go ahead and wait for me at the bottom."

For a moment she hesitated, a tall slim figure faintly silhouetted against the last glow of the dying fire behind them. He put his hands on her shoulders, holding her and comforting her. She was a level-headed, capable girl, not given to easy fears, but he knew—because he was not untouched by it himself—how the gloom of this cave, the sensation of being trapped, of having to work in the darkness, could heighten fears.

"We'll get out. Don't worry. The draught up that funnel is too strong to mean that there isn't an opening."

He reached forward and kissed her and for a moment she came to him, held close to him, the two of them taking comfort from each other.

Then she was on her hands and knees, and flat to the ground began to work her way into the tunnel. When she had disappeared, Sinclair went back to the fire and the piled rocks which marked Hadlow's grave. He stamped his foot on the last of the fire after he had pulled aside the piled rocks and from then on he worked in the darkness, using his sense of touch. He worked, deliberately shutting all thought from his mind.

A few moments later he was wriggling his own way through the tunnel, dragging his rifle with him, and inside one of the large pockets of his bush shirt was the body belt which Hadlow had been wearing.

Nina went first up the funnel. Sinclair followed close behind her, ready in case she slipped, the rifle slung over his shoulder. The sides of the funnel were rough and creviced and it was not difficult to get foot and hand holds. They climbed in darkness, groping ahead of them, and as they went up Sinclair realised that the funnel was getting narrower and narrower. Finally it was so narrow that they could climb it like a rock chimney with their backs pressed against one wall and their feet against another. Above him, as he climbed, he would now and then touch Nina's foot and when she stopped to rest then he stopped. When they had gone about forty yards, though it was difficult to keep any track of distance in the dark, he heard her give a sudden exclamation. Reaching up he could not feel her above him. He climbed on and then felt his head touch rock above him. At the same time a hand came back and found his. He was pulled forward and the next moment was being helped over a shelf of rock where the funnel broke away at a sudden right angle. He lay on a wide ledge, Nina at his side, and her voice came to him excitedly.

"Look, Bill! Look!"

Flat on the rock he raised his head and looked forward. Some way ahead there was light, a faint, pallid loom of light that caught the sharp edge of a rock. Then, as his eyes focused after the blackness, the light seemed to increase. They were at the end of a tunnel little bigger than the one which had brought them to the foot of the funnel. The air about them now was fresh and a few yards ahead of them Sinclair saw the clean-picked whitened bones of a small deer-like animal. The sight stirred his hopes.

They were going to make it.  If a deer could get in, then they could get out.

*          *          *

They came out through a small opening between two rocks which were screened by bushes.  They stood up, two figures torn and scratched, filthy with their work in the cave, and there before them was the long sweep of mountain running down from the far side of the great pile of rocks.  Sinclair put down his rifle and turned to Nina.  She was pale and tired looking but she was smiling.  Then, as she moved towards him, Mabenge stepped out from the far side of the bushes.  He held a carbine in his hands, levelled at them, and behind him was N'Dene—N'Dene who had escaped long ago from this cave in the same way.

Mabenge said, "If you make one wrong step I shall use this."  The tip of the carbine muzzle moved and he came forward.

Nina said, "Mabenge, what's all this about?"

Mabenge shook his head.  "Don't let us waste time on idle questions.  This man knows what I want.  And he would never have left the cave without it.  N'Dene—in his pocket."

N'Dene came forward.  This was his moment, this morning had been full of great moments.

He went up to Sinclair, and Sinclair saw the can opener he had presented to him strung on a thong about his neck.  N'Dene put out his good left hand and jerked the belt free from the shirt pocket.

Sinclair, watching Mabenge, feeling a great bitterness at the way all his efforts were ending, said "It seems that I've had a lot of work for nothing."  All the time he was watching, watching Mabenge and the tip of the carbine.

N'Dene backed away and then turned and held out the belt to Mabenge.

Close to his side Sinclair felt Nina's hand take his arm, and he knew that she wanted to restrain him, and he knew equally well that a man like himself couldn't be restrained because the power was not there. At this moment the issue was simplified to the point of a straightforward gamble. Mabenge wanted the diamonds and he wanted them. They would go to the better man.

N'Dene said to Mabenge, "Into your hands, O Mabenge, as the oracle spoke. And it is I, N'Dene, who bring about this thing." He lowered his head and held the belt forward. Mabenge put out his right hand and took the belt to put it inside his battledress jacket and in that simple, unconscious movement came Sinclair's chance because for a few seconds Mabenge's right hand was away from the trigger guard of the carbine. He flung himself forward and swept with his right arm violently at the carbine barrel. The blow jerked the carbine sideways and Sinclair crashed with his full weight into Mabenge. For a moment Mabenge's great body resisted the blow, then he staggered back, lost his balance, and they went down together. The carbine and Hadlow's belt dropped to the ground as the two men rolled over and over.

Before N'Dene could move Nina jumped forward and picked up the carbine and the belt. She whipped round and covered N'Dene, seeing out of the corner of her eye, the struggling pair of men. She backed away and reached for Sinclair's rifle from the ground. She picked it up and slung it over her shoulder. N'Dene watched her, his lips working in silent anger.

For Sinclair, twisting and struggling on the ground, came the moment of certainty that, although he had seized his advantage, he could never develop it. Mabenge was twice as strong as he was, a rolling, jerking mass of muscle and power. Sinclair got his hands on the man's wrists and tried to hold him but his grip was jerked away and Mabenge's fists began to smash at him. Then one hand came up, grabbing at Sinclair's face, the big, widespread fingers seeking his eyes. He squirmed away, throwing Mabenge's weight from him and they rolled, locked together, and then the roll was suddenly a long slide and they went over the edge of a small drop. For a fraction of a second Sinclair saw the hard rock ground coming up to him and he twisted violently and the movement flung him clear from Mabenge. He hit the ground with his shoulder and rolled to a stop. Momentarily he lay there, winded and incapable of more effort. Slowly he pulled himself up and it was to see Mabenge stretched out on the rock, the great body sprawled slackly, unmoving.

Nina came jumping down to him, shouting to him, and in a daze he was on his feet and taking the carbine from her. N'Dene stood on the rock ledge above them, staring down at Mabenge. He seemed unaware of the others. Mabenge lay still and the grey surface of the rock near his head was suddenly dark with the flow of blood.

Nina went over to him and turned his head. As she did so, Mabenge groaned and moved a little.

"He's all right. Cracked his head."

A few moments later they were going hard up the mountain side, heading for the plateau. Behind them N'Dene was at Mabenge's side. He had the Azande's head on his knees and was rocking it gently, muttering to himself, and unable to beat away the great confusion which was in his mind. Looking down he saw Mabenge's eyes flutter open, shut again and then open once more, staring straight up at him. Blood from his head wound had splattered on to the breast of his green battledress jacket and N'Dene saw that in the fight the little black patch in the shape of a flamingo on the breast had been ripped away. All that remained now was its mark on the cloth, a faded shadow that looked almost white.

Mabenge's lips moved and he said faintly, "O N'Dene the oracle spoke the truth, the bare truth, for it said that my hands should hold the diamonds and this they did . . . they held them. . . ."

# CHAPTER FIFTEEN

THE morning now was in its first flush of beauty, high mackerel-scaled clouds with their bellies tinged with gold and pink streamed away to the west, and below them the grey bare mountain slopes and shoulders had turned a hard, sugar white under the blaze. In the distance spread the vast reaches of forest and jungle. Some impulse made Sinclair put the Auster's nose up and climb, and he had a feeling that he would like to go on climbing.

Behind him he could hear Amra grunting with pleasure and at his side, from the corner of his eye, he could see Nina doing things with her hair, using her hands adroitly and then wiping her face with a crumpled square of handkerchief which she had produced from somewhere.

The whole thing, he told himself, had been simple. You kept your head down and never stopped going and in the end things had to break for you. It had been an awkward moment coming out of the mountainside and finding Mabenge and N'Dene waiting, but luck had played with him. He was strong enough, but nothing like as strong as Mabenge and the Azande could have broken him easily if time had been granted to him. And after that, when they had reached the plateau, convinced now that his luck must hold, he had had no qualms when he had seen the guard by the plane. From a hundred yards he had fired, taking cover with Nina behind a boulder, and he had fired for the ground at the man's side. Two shots . . . and the guard not seeing him had begun to fire wildly back; and then Amra had opened fire from the cover of the woods and suddenly the guard, harassed by unseen enemies, had taken to his heels and run for the cover of the far trees. Three minutes later the Auster was airborne,

and now here they were, flying high, wide and handsome,
enough petrol in the tanks to take him three hundred
miles at least . . . and at his side Nina.

He banked the plane round towards the north and now,
tired of the height, eased the nose down gently.

Nina said, "Where are you going?"

"I don't know. Any suggestions?"

"It depends, doesn't it?"

"On what?"

"On what you want to do."

"That depends, too, doesn't it?"

"On what?"

"On what you decide to do. You've finished with your
step-father?"

"Of course. I see now that he was just getting odder and
odder. This thing was eating into him."

"He and Mabenge may still go on trying."

"They've missed the boat."

"You'll let the authorities know what they are up to?"

"I don't know. No, I don't think I will. I couldn't do
that to him, despite everything."

"Without money the whole thing will fizzle."

Ahead of them suddenly, coming up at a different angle
was the lake. They were coming in from the south-east
with N'Dene's homestead tucked away under their left
hand and the long run of blinding white sands dancing
with the first heat haze beyond the shallow spread of
rippling, silver water. The morning flight of the flamingoes
was long over, but there was a certain amount of movement in the birds still, little parties winging their way low
over the surface, and near the shore larger parties were
wading and feeding.

Nina put her hand out and opened the side window of
the cockpit a little. Air rushed in carrying with it the
louder beat of the engine. Sinclair saw her lean back in
her seat and breathe deeply. The movement tightened
the line of her throat and the draught caught at her fair

hair and blew it back from her temples and her profile was clean and beautiful.

He said, "I love you, Nina."

Behind them Amra grunted.

Then Nina said, "And I love you—but where does that get us?"

"It's all we need, isn't it?"

"No." She turned towards him slowly, and then went on, her voice touched with exasperation, "For God's sake, Bill—let's drop the fencing and be honest. You've got to make up your mind and this time you've got to make the right decision."

"I'm not with you."

"Oh, yes you are. You know perfectly well what I'm getting at. You've got the diamonds and you want to keep them. If I know you, you've convinced yourself now that they really do belong to you after all you've done for them. You've got them, and you want me. And that's what makes it so bloody awful for me."

"What's wrong with keeping the stuff? You and I can use it. And we'll be together."

"I see . . ." Nina was silent for a moment, thinking. Then she gave a little laugh. "Well, I suppose I'll have to risk it."

"There's no great risk."

"Not the kind of risk you're thinking about. Most of what you are, I like. I've shown you that long ago. But I can see that I've got to do something about the part I don't like. That's where the risk comes in. It could put you against me for good."

"Sometimes you talk in riddles."

"This is no riddle." She reached down to where Hadlow's belt lay at her feet and picked it up with her left hand.

"What the devil are you doing?"

"Taking a risk." Her right hand rested on his arm.

As Sinclair put the nose up gently to take the heights

beyond the lake, the camp flashing by beneath them, Nina put her left hand out of the cockpit and the belt with its buttoned pouches streamed in the air.

"Haul that thing back in here. Have you gone off your head?"

"No. It's staying there. It's going to stay there all the way to Bisaka. But you go off course and I'll reach over and undo the pouches and let the whole lot go scattering."

He half turned and looked at her. Her face was serious, lips tight, and her blue eyes were defiant. He knew that she meant what she said.

"Somebody's got to change your bloody stupid mind for you," she said.

Momentarily he was furious with her and then, seeing her smile triumphantly, he found himself smiling too.

"You're taking a damned big risk."

"I know."

"You want me to land at Bisaka, be a good boy, hand the stuff over to Suchard, and live happily ever after?"

"Yes. Happily ever after! I'd risk anything for that. This is the only way, you big fool of a man!"

He began to laugh then. He threw his head back and laughed and it was good laughter, coming from a freedom and lightness inside him which was like a great shiver of exultation.

"O.K. you win. Now bring the thing inside. I'll be a good boy."

She put up her free right hand and touched his face and he turned and kissed her hand. But she said, "I believe you, but I don't trust you. My hand stays out there until we reach Bisaka, cramp or no cramp."

Behind them Amra grunted and then said, "Boss, you going to make things right with Mr. Voyadis for me? I get hell for fixing up this plane for you."

"Don't worry, Amra. We'll fix things up. That's the beauty about things, they can always be fixed up someway."

He swung left handed and out of the green tree maze below the long, lazy brown loops of the Bomu came up. He put out his hand and rested it on the nape of Nina's neck, feeling the warmth of the brown skin, not looking at her, just content with the smoothness of her skin under his hard palm.

Not far ahead of them now was Bisaka. He thought of Nahud, imagining the man's surprise when he would walk in with the diamonds . . . anxious little Nahud . . . a hundred and fifty feddans of land, and a new wife . . . everyone had to have a dream, and sometimes the dream came true. Nina put up her free hand and laid it over his.